Saddle Up and Ride

Carol Lynne

Reining in the Past

When Ray Justice receives a phone call that his father has died, he's shocked. As far as he knew, his father passed away twenty-three years earlier. Adding to the confusion, he finds that he's inherited a large cattle ranch in Montana.

Alfred Deacon came to the J Bar Ranch as a broken cowboy in search of acceptance and honest work. What he found was a best friend and a group of cowboys he'd do anything for. When Ray walks into his life, Deacon is torn between loyalties to his dead friend and desire so strong it makes him weak.

Ray comes face-to-face with a past he didn't know he had and a man he didn't know he needed.

Bareback Cowboy

Ethan Griggs is quite happy living on Justice River Ranch. He spends his days as head wrangler, tending to the horses he loves and the guests he's learned to tolerate. When Bridger Collins arrives at the ranch, Griggs' world is turned upside down. Despite his usual hands-off policy with the guests, he's immediately drawn to the younger man.

Bridger thrives on the cowboy way of life. The son of one of the richest men in the country, Bridger would rather fix a fence than sit behind a desk counting his money. The sexual chemistry he seems to share with Griggs is simply icing on the cake.

With his week-long stay coming to a close, Bridger is forced to choose between the life he wants with Griggs and the life planned for him since birth.

An Ellora's Cave Publication

www.ellorascave.com

Saddle Up and Ride

ISBN 9781419966507
ALL RIGHTS RESERVED.
Reining in the Past Copyright © 2009 Carol Lynne
Bareback Cowboy Copyright © 2010 Carol Lynne
Edited by Meghan Conrad.
Design by Irene Adler and Syneca
Photography by shutterstock.com and fotolia.com.

Trade paperback publication 2012

With the exception of quotes used in reviews, this book may not be reproduced or used in whole or in part by any means existing without written permission from the publisher, Ellora's Cave Publishing, Inc.® 1056 Home Avenue, Akron OH 44310-3502.

Warning: The unauthorized reproduction or distribution of this copyrighted work is illegal. Criminal copyright infringement, including infringement without monetary gain, is investigated by the FBI and is punishable by up to 5 years in federal prison and a fine of $250,000. (http://www.fbi.gov/ipr/)

This book is a work of fiction and any resemblance to persons, living or dead, or places, events or locales is purely coincidental. The characters are productions of the author's imagination and used fictitiously.

The publisher and author(s) acknowledge the trademark status and trademark ownership of all trademarks, service marks and word marks mentioned in this book.

The publisher does not have any control over and does not assume any responsibility for author or third-party Web sites or their content.

SADDLE UP AND RIDE
Carol Lynne

ಖ

REINING IN THE PAST
~9~

BAREBACK COWBOY
~93~

REINING IN THE PAST

Dedication

To the owners and staff of the Lazy E L Ranch in Roscoe, Montana. Thank you for one of the best weeks of my life.

Chapter One

Ray Justice looked from the daunting stack of papers to the setting sun out the large window of his office. There was a time when he was under the impression that once you became established in your job, the work evened out. Not so, at least not for employees of Brockway, Lee and Thompson.

The advertising firm was one of the top in the nation and Ray was riding a pretty impressive wave of awards for his ad campaigns. His gaze moved to the dormant drafting table on the opposite side of the room. He was paid a hefty salary to come up with new and innovative campaigns, so why was the majority of his day spent doing paperwork?

His ringing cell phone broke up his little self-absorbed pity party. He frowned at the caller display, not recognizing the long distance number. "Probably a damn telemarketer," he mumbled. Still, a phone call was better than tackling the rest of the waiting paperwork.

"Ray Justice," he answered, swinging his feet to the top of his glass and chrome desk.

"Raymond Eli Justice, Jr.?"

"Yes. May I help you?"

"My name is James Krueger, from the Law Office of Krueger and Westmoor in Red Lodge, Montana. I'm representing your late father's estate and I was hoping to set up a meeting with you after his funeral."

Ray stifled a gasp before it could escape. "I'm sorry, you must have the wrong Ray Justice. My father died over twenty-three years ago."

"Are you Raymond Eli Justice, born in West Seneca, New York, January 23, 1982?"

"Yes, that's me, but like I've already told you, my father died when I was three." He almost hung up on the guy. Ray hadn't discussed his namesake since he was seven years old and had made his mother cry.

"I'm sorry to be the one to inform you this, but Raymond Eli Justice, Sr., died two days ago on his ranch in Montana."

* * * * *

Still numb from his earlier conversation, Ray pulled his car into the small detached garage and turned off the engine. His gaze settled on the tools over the workbench to his left. Lined up like soldiers, the tools had been the only things he had that were his father's.

Ray took pride in making sure they were maintained in a way that would make his dad proud. Getting out of the low-slung sports car, he ran a hand over the sharp, oiled implements that he'd never learned to use. *Why had he left them?*

With a sigh, Ray turned and grabbed his briefcase out of the passenger seat. After locking up the garage, he let himself into his boyhood home. Everything looked somehow different to him.

It had been over eight years since his mother's death and very little about the house had changed. Ray tossed his keys onto the yellow Formica and chrome table and headed upstairs to the attic.

If his mother had secrets he'd uncover them in the boxes she'd kept stored in the seldom-visited space. Using a chair from his desk, Ray grabbed the short cord of the trap door and pulled. The rusty hinges gave a squeal as the ladder began to unfold. He hopped off the chair and settled the bottom of the ladder against the scarred wooden floor.

He wasn't sure what he'd find in the old trunks, but something told him his life was about to change.

* * * * *

Ray bent over his mother's grave and removed stray debris from the simple headstone. When Isabella Justice had passed away, Ray had still been in college and unable to afford anything elaborate. Now the stone shamed him. He earned a tidy sum, so why hadn't he thought to repay his mom for all the years of hard work she'd performed in his name?

"I finally dug through all those old boxes you had stored."

He leaned back on his heels and stuck his hands in his jacket pockets. "Why didn't you tell me? Why lie all these years?"

The divorce papers he'd found in his mother's attic had been a surprise discovery. He'd spent the remainder of the evening trying to come to terms with his mother's betrayal.

He started to walk off, but stopped and turned back. "Maybe you were just trying to protect me. I get that, really I do. But don't you think I deserved to know my dad was still alive? Or was it easier for you to think of him as being dead?"

Ray sighed and studied the surrounding grave markers. "I'm taking some time off. Hell, I'm not sure I'll even have a job to come back to, but I need to go. His funeral's Monday and for some reason, I think it's important for me to be there. I don't know why, maybe I'm going to spit on his grave, or maybe just for the chance to see what was more important to him than we were."

* * * * *

Ray tossed the map onto the passenger seat and made a left. He drove under the large J Bar Ranch sign and with sweating palms. When he'd stopped in the small town of Red

Lodge for directions, the guy seemed to know just where Ray needed to go. Was the J Bar that well known?

He winced as the undercarriage of his rented luxury sedan scraped against the rutted dirt road. *Good thing I took the added insurance.* He crested a rolling hill and gasped as the J Bar came into view, buildings of all sizes laid out in a storybook valley below. *Crap.* He'd wanted to hate the place, but how could anyone not see the beauty of the ranch?

He noticed a group of cowboys gathered around the largest barn and pulled up close to them. A press of a button and the driver's side window slid smoothly down. "Excuse me. Are any of you Alfred Deacon?"

A young cowboy chuckled. "Alfred? Is that Deacon's first name?" The man turned back to his friends. "Hell, boys, we've got some teasin' to do."

The majority of the cowboys were laughing as they walked off. Ray couldn't believe they were going to just ignore his initial question. "I take it he's not here."

One of the men stepped closer to the car and pointed toward the barn. "You'll find Deacon in the tack room. He's always the last one to show up for lunch."

"Thanks." Ray rolled up the window and turned off the engine. He watched through the rearview mirror as the group of cowboys walked into a small building across the dirt road.

With a deep breath, Ray climbed out of the car and reached back inside for his suit jacket. After attempting to get as many wrinkles out of his charcoal gray pants as he could, he entered the barn. He glanced around. *What the hell is a tack room?*

"Hello? Mr. Deacon?"

"Back here," a deep voice responded.

Ray grinned for the first time in two days. Alfred Deacon's voice sounded exactly like one of those cowboys from the movies, low and gravelly, like Deacon had smoked too many cigarettes in his lifetime.

He walked to the back of the barn and down a slight slope into what he assumed was the tack room. Ray's first glimpse of his father's ranch manager surprised him. Deacon appeared to be in his mid-thirties, much younger than Ray would've guessed, and gorgeous. "Mr. Deacon?"

Deacon glanced up from the saddle he was working on. "Fuck."

Ray's eyes rounded. "Excuse me?"

Deacon shook his head and walked toward Ray, hand extended. "Sorry. You threw me there for a second. You're the spitting image of your dad."

Ray shifted uncomfortably. "I wouldn't know."

Deacon stopped and dropped his hand to the side. "Yeah. I guess you wouldn't. Sorry about that."

Ray shrugged. Sympathy was something he'd never felt comfortable with and for some reason, getting it from the six-foot-four gorgeous cowboy with dark chocolate eyes made it even worse.

Now it was Deacon's turn to look uncomfortable. He hooked his thumb in his front pocket and nodded toward the doorway. "You eaten?"

Ray shook his head. "I came straight from the airport in Billings. I wasn't sure how long it would take and I wanted to make sure I made it here before dark."

Chuckling, Deacon waved for Ray to follow him. "This is Montana, not the end of the earth. Although some winters when the snow reaches the roofline, it starts to feel like it. Why don't you join me for lunch in the cookhouse?"

"Okay, if you think no one will mind."

"Mind? Hell, you own the place now. After lunch I'll take you over to the main house and help get you settled." Deacon climbed the steps to the small building he'd seen the cowboys enter earlier. He stopped and poured some steaming water into a bowl and began to wash his hands in the makeshift sink.

After Deacon was finished, he stepped back. Ray wasn't sure if he was expected to wash his hands or not, but decided to follow suit just in case. He took off his suit jacket and glanced around for a place to hang it.

"I'll take it."

"Thanks." Ray handed off the jacket and rolled up his sleeves before mimicking the procedure Deacon had used.

"Do you mind telling me how my father died?" Ray asked.

"You don't know?"

Ray shook his head. "I was just told he died."

"One of the hands found him down by the river. He'd evidently had a heart attack, fell from his horse and hit his head on a rock."

"So what killed him, the heart attack or the fall?"

Deacon shrugged. "Doesn't much matter. Dead is dead."

Once Ray's hands were dry, he reached for his jacket.

"That's okay. I'll hang it up for you." Deacon opened the screen door and walked through a small mudroom where he stopped to hang the expensive jacket on a wooden peg.

Ray winced at the thought of the thousand-dollar piece of clothing being treated like an ordinary denim jacket. He followed Deacon into the large room filled with long tables lined with chairs.

"I'd like you all to meet Ray Justice, Jr.," Deacon introduced him.

Half the jaws in the room dropped. The cowboys began firing off questions.

"What? RJ had a son?"

"Why didn't we know that?" another man asked.

Deacon held up his hands and shook his head. "RJ didn't do anything without good reason and you know that. Now stop acting like a bunch of jackasses and introduce yourselves."

The first young cowboy he'd spoken to on the ranch stepped forward, his hand extended. "I'm Cody Williams. Been working at the J Bar for close to six years. I handle the guests."

Ray shook the man's hand. "Guests? I thought this was a cattle ranch?"

"We open the ranch up to paid guests from the end of May through mid-October. Ranching alone isn't enough anymore to make a spread of this size profitable, so we use the added revenue the guests bring in to keep us afloat," Deacon explained.

Ray glanced around the room. "So where are the guests? Do they eat in another dining hall or something?"

"Nope. They eat right here with us. The last batch left this morning. We've got another small group coming in tomorrow," Deacon further explained.

Another cowboy stood up. "Hi, Ray. I'm Neil, the J Bar cowboss. I help coordinate the grazing fields with the manager, uh, that'd be Deacon. I also take some of the guests along to put out minerals for the cattle and stuff like that."

"Neil sells himself short," Deacon butted in. "He's also the best damn roper I've ever known, as well as field vet for the cattle out in the pastures."

A handsome man with dark red hair stood and touched the bill of his baseball cap. "I'm Jimmy. I only work the summer months. I'm a student at the University of Montana. While I'm here, I help with a little of everything, from taking guests on trail rides to helping move head from one pasture to another."

"Pleased to meet you." Ray glanced at Deacon. "Head?"

"Ranching term for cattle."

Ray nodded, feeling like an idiot. "Of course."

"And Griggs is our head horse wrangler. He's also the only cowboy you're likely to see with a ponytail."

Ray grinned and shook the Native American's hand. "Pleased to meet you."

"Likewise."

Deacon went on to introduce a few more of the wranglers. "We've also got some part-timers who're out mowing and readying the cabins for the arrival of our guests in the morning."

A woman came out of the kitchen drying her hands on a small towel. "If you two don't stop flapping your jaws and eat, everything will be colder than a well digger's ass."

Deacon chuckled. "And the vision of loveliness behind the counter is our weekend cook, Libby. During the week, Martha is the regular cook. Martha's known to everyone as Mother. When we have guests on hand, she has an assistant, Donna, who comes in to help. Other than that, it looks like all we're missing is Beth, who runs the office, Taggert, who's attending his little brother's football game, and the few part-timers spread out doing chores. I'll introduce you to them later."

Deacon picked up a plate and handed it to Ray. "We serve all the food buffet-style, so help yourself. If there's something in particular you want, just ask Libby or Mother. They're usually pretty accommodating."

Ray filled his plate with salad, some green beans and the smallest piece of fried chicken he could find before sitting in one of the empty chairs.

Deacon's long legs straddled the chair next to Ray as he settled in with his heaping plate of food. He glanced at Ray's plate and shook his head. "Not sure that little plate of food is gonna get you through 'til supper."

"I normally don't eat lunch, so I'm sure I'll be fine." Ray ate a large bite of his salad, impressed with the ranch dressing—it definitely hadn't come out of a bottle.

Deacon reached for the basket of rolls and set it between them. "I'll fill you in on more of the basics once we get you settled."

Ray nodded. He removed the skin from his chicken and ate a small piece of the meat. "So how many cows does this place have?"

"We don't call them cows, remember? They're cattle or head."

"Sorry. Guess I have a lot to learn. I've never even been on a horse, except the kind at the fair that go 'round and 'round in a circle."

Jimmy snorted and Deacon shot him a reprimanding look. "Well, you came to the right place to learn. We've got horses for all skill levels. Later I'll introduce you to a few of my favorites."

"I need to call my father's attorney and let him know I'm here. He wants me to come by his office in Red Lodge after the funeral on Monday. Is that where the funeral will be, in Red Lodge?"

"Yes and no. Visitation is tomorrow night in Red Lodge at RJ's favorite bar, but the burial will be here on the ranch, Monday morning."

"Here?"

Deacon nodded as he swallowed a bite of food. "The J Bar has been in the Justice family for four generations, you make it five. There's a small family cemetery up on the ridge. Shallow Valley's on one side, the ranch buildings on the other."

Four generations? Ray hadn't even met his grandparents on his mother's side. He couldn't imagine having something stay in a family for four generations. And five? Ray knew that wasn't going to happen. His life was back east, not in Montana.

Before he could tell Deacon, the handsome man spoke again. "There's been an outfit out of Billings that have been trying to buy the place for several years. I'll bet they'll be shocked as hell to find out a fifth-generation Justice has shown up. I'm sure that's partly what James Krueger wants to talk to you about."

Ray pushed his plate away. What little appetite he'd had was gone. He knew he needed to tell Deacon the truth. "Well, to be honest. The ranch might do better in someone else's hands. I work in marketing. I don't know the first thing about running a place like this. I thought I'd ask Mr. Krueger to find a buyer for the ranch."

Deacon set down his fork and turned to face Ray. "I'm hoping you'll reconsider. The people who're interested in buying want to put up a resort complete with hotels, apartments and condos. There won't be any 'ranch' left after they're finished. And as far as the ranch goes, you don't need to know how to run it. You've got people who can do that for you."

Although Ray knew he wasn't going to change his mind, he couldn't tell Deacon in a roomful of men who depended on the ranch for their livelihood. "I'll think about it."

*****

Deacon unlocked the ornately carved front door of the main house and led the way inside. "Well, this is it. You've got four bedrooms upstairs, including the master. It's your house now."

Ray looked around the room. A photograph on the fireplace caught his attention. He walked over and lifted it off the mantel. It was a small group of men and women. "You keep saying things like that, but none of this feels like mine. I don't know any of the people in this photograph. I mean, I know this one is my father, but only because I found a picture of him in my mom's attic yesterday."

Deacon walked over within reach of the picture. "The older man is your grandpa, Ben, and that's your grandma,

Gloria. I'm not real sure, but I think those other two men worked for your grandpa."

Ray glanced over his shoulder. "Do you know why he did it? Why he left us...me?"

"Not really. He said something once when he was drunk that always had me wondering though."

"What'd he say?" Ray gazed at the image of his father. Although RJ's hair was cut in a different style, Ray could tell he also had the same unruly mess that had plagued him his entire life. In the black-and-white photograph, Ray couldn't tell if they shared the same green eyes. Ray figured they did since his mom's had been blue. He reached up and absently ran his fingers over the deep dimple in his left cheek. Just like Ray, RJ had a dimple on the left side of his face.

"He said if he'd had his life to do over again, he'd have done a lot of things differently."

Ray put the picture back on the mantel. "Did he ever talk about me?"

Deacon rested a hand on Ray's shoulder. "Once a year, toward the end of January, he'd lock himself in the house and go on a three- or four-day bender."

Ray bit his bottom lip. Had his father remembered? "My birthday's January 23rd."

"I figured as much, once he finally told me about you," Deacon admitted.

Deacon knew about me? "When was that?"

"A little more than three years ago, I'd guess." Deacon picked up an old baseball from the mantel.

"Can you tell me what he said about me?" Ray asked, taking the ball from Deacon and putting it back in its holder.

"Wasn't nothin', really. He just let it slip that his son was graduating college," Deacon said.

Ray was shocked. "He knew I went to college? How?"

Deacon shrugged. "Who knows."

With his hands clasped behind his back, Ray walked away. He couldn't explain his feelings. A large part of him was pissed that his father had dared pry into his life enough to learn about important events, events that he'd celebrated alone after the death of his mother. Yet there was a small part of him that was touched that at least his father cared in his own small, selfish way.

Without turning to face Deacon, Ray asked, "Do you think it would be too intrusive if I looked around a bit? Maybe I can find a clue as to why he did what he did."

A set of keys were tossed onto the table at Ray's side.

"Those were his. A few of the smaller ones look like they go to his desk," Deacon informed him.

Ray picked up the keys and regarded the suddenly sullen man. "You seem mad."

"I guess I am, but not at you. I mean, I don't begrudge you trying to get to know your family, it just seems weird to have someone else in his house. RJ was my best friend for over thirteen years. I guess it's hard for me to believe he's gone," Deacon said.

Maybe he'd been wrong about the ranch manager's age. "You don't look that old."

Deacon grinned. "I'm not, really. I just turned thirty-two."

"So you've known RJ since you were nineteen?" Ray asked.

"No. I said I've considered him my best friend since I was nineteen. I've actually known him since I was fifteen. I'm a local boy. I worked here in the summers. After I graduated, I knew I wanted to find a job on a ranch, but RJ didn't have any full-time positions open. So I went looking and finally found a job up north."

Deacon walked over to the mantel and picked up a picture of RJ on a horse. "Things...didn't work out. I came back here and RJ created a job for me. Over the years, I was able to work my way up to manager." Deacon glanced around the room. "I've spent a lot of time in here over the years."

"Would you feel better about all this if you stayed while I opened my father's desk?"

Deacon settled his cowboy hat back on his head and walked to the door. "No, I don't think so. I appreciate you asking, but if RJ wanted me to know his secrets, he would've told me."

His hand on the doorknob, Deacon turned back to Ray. "My house is the one next to the barn. When you're ready, I'll introduce you to those horses we talked about. You might as well get your first lesson in before the new guests arrive in the morning."

"Thanks," Ray said.

Deacon tipped his hat and walked out the door.

Ray shut the door and leaned back against it. His gaze traveled the large, rustically furnished room. He tried to picture his father lounging on the leather sofa, his closely cropped black and gray hair resting on one of the tapestry pillows.

Everything he'd heard about his father since he'd stepped foot on the ranch was in complete contrast to the man who'd abandoned him so long ago. Without even realizing it, Ray slowly walked toward the couch. Studying the father who was only visible in his imagination, Ray wiped tears from his eyes. "Who are you?"

Chapter Two

Ray sat at the large antique desk that had belonged to four generations of Justice men. His hands shook as he held what he knew was the key that would unlock more clues to his past. With a deep breath, he reached down and fit the key into the small brass lock.

It wasn't until he'd searched the bottom drawer that he found something more personal than checkbooks and account balances. He pulled out the old shoebox and set it on the desktop.

Ray wasn't sure how long he stared at the box, marked with his name written in his father's hand. He traced the pen strokes with the tip of his finger. Getting up, Ray crossed the masculine study to the small bar and poured himself a shot of whiskey. Drinking wasn't something he usually indulged in, but he needed all the strength he could muster. If it had to come out of a bottle, so be it.

He returned to the desk and blew out a calming breath as he lifted the faded cardboard lid. He rubbed his eyes as he stared down at a stack of letters, tons of them. He quickly flipped through the top four or five envelopes and shook his head. *What the hell?*

* * * * *

A loud knock on the front door drew Ray's attention. He blinked several times and wiped his eyes. As he stood, opened letters drifted to the floor. The carpet around his feet was littered with them.

He stepped over the stack and made his way to the door. When he opened it, he was surprised to see it was dark outside.

Deacon held out a foil-covered plate. "You missed dinner."

Still in a daze, Ray took the plate. "Thanks."

"Are you okay?" Deacon asked.

Ray shook his head. "No." He glanced toward the study. "Can I show you something?"

Deacon nodded and followed Ray into RJ's office. Ray set the plate of food on the desk and gestured to the letters and envelopes strewn across the floor. "They were all addressed to me, but only a few of them had ever been mailed."

Deacon bent over and lifted a small stack of papers. Before he began reading, he looked at Ray. "Is this okay with you?"

"Yeah. Maybe you can answer a few questions for me."

Still holding the papers in his hand, Deacon glanced around the room. "How many of them are there?"

Ray shrugged. "I didn't count, sixty, seventy maybe. It looks like he wrote two or three a year, usually one at my birthday, sometimes one at Christmas and one every year on June seventeenth. It must've been around the time he left. There was even a Return to Sender envelope. It was a high school graduation card."

Ray picked up a letter and handed it to Deacon. "This one's actually from my mother."

Deacon took the letter.

As Deacon read the lies that Ray's mother had written, Ray shifted uncomfortably. He still couldn't believe he'd been betrayed by the one person in the world he'd thought he could count on.

Deacon finished reading and handed the paper back to Ray. "Did you really feel this way?"

Exasperated, Ray threw up his hands. "She told me he was dead. Of course I didn't tell her I wanted nothing to do with him."

Ray dropped to the floor and ran his hands over the letters. "I can't understand why he'd believe her."

Deacon cleared his throat and sat on the floor beside Ray. "RJ was gay. It's not uncommon for people to hate someone based solely on their sexual preference. According to what your mom wrote, you were disgusted by him and continually wished he was dead."

"My father was gay? Well, I guess that explains a few things."

Deacon put his hand on Ray's thigh. "Like?"

Ray shook his head. "Her snide comments about queers. How she reacted when I came out to her after high school."

"You're…"

"Yep. I knew it most of my life, but I didn't dare tell her while I was still living at home. We didn't really talk much after that. She said I was lucky my dad's money was paying… Shit! I can't believe I didn't think of it before. Mom said Dad's money was paying for my college. I thought she meant some kind of life insurance policy or something. Damn. That's how he knew when I graduated."

Ray stood and began to pace around the study. What had his father thought of him? "I bet he thought he had a real prize for a son. Some snot-nosed brat who refused to see him yet gladly took his money. No wonder the later letters aren't nearly as kind as the early ones. He must've hated me."

Deacon stepped in front of him and stopped the pacing with a hand on Ray's chest. "Don't beat yourself up over it. It wasn't your fault."

Ray reached up and grabbed a handful of his spiky black hair, giving it a sharp tug. It was something he'd done since he was a child, a way of punishing himself. "I wish I could tell him. He died thinking I hated him."

Deacon removed Ray's fingers from his hair. "What? You don't think he's looking down on us at this very moment? Well, I knew RJ and I can tell you without a doubt, he's listenin' to every word we say. He never did like people talking behind his back."

Ray looked at his hand surrounded by Deacon's much bigger one. He hated himself for being a weak nelly in front of the tough rancher. His hand in Deacon's felt almost...cherished. What would it feel like to be totally surrounded by the manager's strong, bronzed body?

Ray quickly pulled away. Although Deacon was definitely his type, he knew thoughts like that could get him hung on a ranch of über-cowboys. "Is it too late to get that riding lesson?"

Deacon looked out the window at the darkness beyond. "It's too late to ride. I'm sure the horses have already been turned out to pasture. If you feel like gettin' an early start in the morning, I can meet you at the barn at five?"

"A.M.?" Ray nearly choked.

Deacon chuckled. "Yep. Breakfast is served at seven and there are chores to be done before then. The guests should arrive right after lunch and we've got the summer cabin to ready."

"Okay. I'll meet you at five. Just don't laugh if I fall asleep on my horse."

* * * * *

Deacon cinched Black Jack's saddle after applying his knee to the large black gelding's stomach. Although a damn fine horse, Black Jack had a tendency to hold air in so the cinch strap didn't fit as tight as it needed to.

He heard the cowboys snickering and glanced around his horse to see what all the commotion was about.

"Damn, even dressed like a city guy, he's hot," Cody drawled.

"Fuck. Who the hell is that walking sugar cube?" Taggert asked. "He's gorgeous."

For some reason Taggert's comment immediately put Deacon into a sour mood. "That's the man who can fire your ass in a heartbeat. So watch your mouth."

He broke away from the cowboys, hollering orders over his shoulder. "Get to work. I want that fence fixed on Logan's Landing before breakfast."

Deacon could hear grumbles as the cowboys mounted and rode out. He'd spent a sleepless night thinking about Ray. Seeing him now with tight jeans and a western-style plaid shirt didn't bode well for the rest of his day. As attracted as he'd been to Ray in a business suit, it didn't hold a candle to the younger man in pretend cowboy gear.

"Sorry I'm late," Ray called out when he was still a few strides away.

"Don't worry about it." Deacon gestured to Ray's crocodile boots. "Those new?"

Ray nodded, a blush creeping up his cheeks. "They are. I admit I didn't have anything appropriate to wear, so I had to go shopping."

"Well, as nice as the boots look, I can't let you wear 'em."

Ray looked down at his shiny new boots. "Why? They're good boots."

Deacon lifted his leg and kicked out. His boot flew off his foot and landed about six feet away. "You need to have on a pair that you can do that with. Otherwise, if you fall out of the saddle and your boot gets caught in the stirrup, the horse'll drag ya."

Ray started to reach for his hair, but seemed to think twice about it. "I don't have any others."

"Don't worry. There's a bunch of old ones down in the cookhouse basement. Quite a few of our guests have the same idea of boots that you do. We'll get ya fixed up after breakfast."

Deacon retrieved his boot before leading Ray to the barn. "I pulled Dandy out for you to try. She's used mainly for the guests, so she knows the ropes."

Ray chuckled. "You mean she's used to city folk on her back."

"Yeah. Something like that." He walked into the tack room and pointed to the rows of saddles perched atop sawhorses. In the center was a long rail used to drape the blankets. "Okay, first thing is to get your blanket and saddle."

Instead of grabbing one off the sawhorse, Deacon ducked into a small side room and came back out with a gorgeous, hand-tooled, cherry-colored saddle. "This one belonged to RJ. I think he'd like it if you were to use it."

Ray ran his hand over the intricately carved initials on the side of the saddle. "Did my father ride Dandy?"

Deacon bit the inside of his cheek to keep from laughing. "No. RJ was one of the best horsemen I've ever known. His mount, Surly, is a little too much for you to handle at this point. Grab that black-and-red-striped blanket from in there, would ya?"

Ray walked into the small room and came back out with RJ's blanket. He didn't say anything, but Deacon could tell it weighed a lot more than Ray was expecting.

Deacon went out the back door and around the corner of the barn where Dandy was tethered to a hitching post. "Okay, throw that blanket up on Dandy's back. Yep, that's it... A little higher up on her neck... Perfect. Now, step back and I'll get this saddle settled. Okay, you take this front cinch here and unhook it from the saddle. Make sure it doesn't swing down and hit your horse though. Just let it fall gently. Then you go over here to this other side and reach under, grab it and hook it through this here rigging. Pull up as hard as you can. I usually give a horse a good nudge with my knee to make sure they aren't puffin' on me. Once you've got it tight enough, just stick this through here. Now, the front cinch should be tight enough that you can barely fit three fingers between it and the horse."

"Is there going to be a test later?" Ray asked with a twinkle in his big green eyes.

Deacon chuckled. "Nope. But unless you want to be tipped on your ass, you'll do it right the first time." Deacon walked behind Ray and maneuvered him to stand beside Dandy. "Now, put your left foot in the stirrup and pull yourself up using the saddle horn. Once you're up, swing your right leg over his rump to the other side."

With his short stature and tight jeans, Ray had a hard time getting his foot in the stirrup. Once it was finally there, Ray was practically doing the splits. Deacon knew there was no way the smaller man would be able to pull himself up. He put both hands on Ray's hips and lifted.

"Swing your leg over," he instructed. He refused to acknowledge how good those tiny hips felt in his hands.

Once he was in the saddle, Ray grinned. "Do I look like a cowboy yet?"

Deacon thought Ray looked like a big slice of heaven from where he stood. "Yep. All you need is a little cowshit on your boots and you'll be set."

"Oh, my boots. Should we change them before we ride?"

Deacon shook his head. "I'm just going to show you the fundamentals for now. We'll do that in one of the riding rings, so you'll be safe."

* * * * *

Before driving to the bar for the memorial service, Deacon took Ray by Jameson's Funeral Home. He parked his battered ranch truck and turned off the engine. "Are you sure about this?"

Ray adjusted his sports jacket. "I'm sure. You don't have to go with me if you don't want, but I need to see him."

Deacon knew he needed to prepare Ray for what he was about to see. There was a reason he'd decided to go with the memorial at the bar instead of one at the funeral home. "When he fell from his horse, his head hit a rock. Lyle Jameson did what he could to hide the damage, but…"

Ray reached across the seat and put his hand on Deacon's. "I understand."

Deacon nodded. The feel of Ray's hand was having a direct effect on his cock. He found himself leaning toward Ray. All he could think about was tasting the man's tempting lips. His elbow hit the horn as he went to pull Ray into his arms, startling them both. *What the hell am I doing?* Deacon thought. Seducing Ray in the parking lot of a funeral home was incredibly stupid. Deacon opened his door and gave Ray the best smile he could muster. "Ready?"

"Yes and no." Ray's eyes appeared to be a tad glazed as he fumbled for the door handle.

Deacon had called ahead and Lyle was waiting just inside the door to take them back.

"I'm sorry for your loss," Lyle said to Ray in greeting.

"Thank you."

Ray followed Lyle into one of the viewing rooms as Deacon hung back. It wasn't that he didn't want to see his old friend, but he thought Ray might need a few minutes alone with his dad first.

Deacon sat at the back of the room and observed Ray, trying to detect what the man was feeling by his posture. He watched as Ray stared at RJ's body for several moments before reaching toward him. Deacon couldn't see what he was doing, but the subtle shake of Ray's shoulders told him the younger man was in distress. He stood and walked up behind Ray, offering a compassionate touch to the grieving man's back. "You doin' okay?"

"He looks so different from what I'd pictured."

Deacon knew Ray wasn't talking about the right side of RJ's head where he'd been dealt the deadly blow. "How so?"

Ray reached out and smoothed the lapel of RJ's black suit. "I don't know. Maybe it's the clothes. They just don't seem to fit him."

"They split the clothes up the back to get them on. You can't expect a tailored fit."

Ray shook his head. "No. That's not what I meant. I see him as more of a jeans and flannel kind of guy."

Deacon grinned. "RJ may have been a rancher, but he was a hell of a dresser when the occasion called for it. He would've wanted to go out in style."

Ray glanced over his shoulder. "Thanks for making sure he'd be happy."

Deacon shrugged. He felt the burn of tears but refused to let them fall. "It's what friends do for each other."

Ray turned around to face Deacon. He reached out and put his hand on Deacon's chest. "I'm sorry. This must be hard on you."

Deacon blinked his eyes, trying to dispel the threatening tears. "It sucks saying goodbye, knowing we'll never share another beer, another laugh." Deacon finally gave up and wiped the moisture from his eyes. "I could've never asked for a better friend."

A tear escaped and Ray quickly reached up to wipe it away. Deacon stared into the green eyes so much like RJ's and felt himself getting lost in them. It would be so easy to bend down and cover those sweet red lips with his own.

Ray seemed to study Deacon for several moments. Suddenly his eyes opened wide. "Were the two of you lovers?"

Surprised, Deacon shook his head. He hadn't mentioned his own sexual preferences to Ray. "No. What makes you think that?"

Ray shrugged. "I don't know. Maybe it's because I can see how much you loved him. I've never cared for a lover that much, let alone a friend. I just thought maybe..."

Deacon shook his head. God, he wanted to kiss Ray, but seducing his best friend's son wasn't something he thought RJ would approve of, especially not right in front of him.

"Can I ask you something?" Ray asked.

"Sure," Deacon answered.

"Are you gay?"

Even after years of being out of the closet on the ranch, it was still hard for Deacon to admit it. "Yes."

"So if you loved my dad, why weren't the two of you lovers?"

"I don't know. We just didn't see each other that way. He wasn't my type, I guess." Deacon knew he needed to change the subject. This wasn't something he wanted to get into with Ray, not there anyway. "Come on. Let's go have a drink in RJ's honor."

* * * * *

Ray unlocked the front door. "I appreciate you taking me."

Deacon stared down at Ray for a few moments. "It was my pleasure."

"Would you like to come in for a drink? Maybe one last toast to my father?" He couldn't explain it, but knew it was important. Ray knew he wasn't the only one feeling the electric current flowing between them.

"I'd better not," Deacon answered.

"Please? Just one? I don't feel like being alone yet."

Deacon eventually nodded and followed Ray into the house. He walked over to the bar and poured them each a glass of whiskey, downing his in one gulp before pouring another. He handed Ray a glass before taking up position beside the fireplace.

Ray took a sip of the strong liquor. "So what time will everyone be here in the morning?"

"We'll meet in front of the barn at nine. It's tradition to ride to the cemetery, but there will also be a van for the older folks. If you'd feel more comfortable riding with them…"

"No. I can ride Dandy. What about the coffin?"

"We'll take it up to the ridge on the buckboard like they've done for generations."

Ray tugged at a strand of hair. "All evening I've been cussing myself out. I sat there and heard all the nice things said about my dad and found myself getting angry at him."

Deacon finished his drink and walked over to pour himself another.

Ray took another sip and set his glass on the table. "God, I wish I could've had him in my life. I spent so many years confused and scared to admit who I was."

Ray knew it was more than that. His dad had built a life he could be proud of. He'd had a fantastic group of friends who supported him at every turn. Ray had never known support like his dad's friends seemed to offer. He walked over to the bar and stood, gazing up into Deacon's dark brown eyes. "I know I don't fit in here, but I want to."

Standing close, Deacon slowly leaned down and brushed his lips across Ray's before quickly pulling back. "I need to go."

Ray watched stunned as Deacon opened the door to leave. The gorgeous man glanced over his shoulder one last time.

"I have stuff to do in the morning. If I'm not around, have one of the guys help you saddle Dandy."

Dammit! Ray wanted to scream as the door shut behind Deacon's broad back. He rushed to the door, intent on going after Deacon, but stopped himself. Whatever demons Deacon was battling, Ray had the feeling it wasn't the time to push the man.

*****

Deacon jumped in his truck and drove the short distance to his small house on the ranch, cussing at himself the entire way. What the hell had he been thinking? He knew as soon as his lips had touched Ray's it had been a mistake.

The attraction went too deep for a casual affair and Ray was his best friend's son. "Fuck!"

He slammed his front door and tore his clothes off on his way to the kitchen to get the unopened bottle of Jack Daniel's RJ had given him for his birthday. Naked, he stood in front of the sink and stared out the window, hoping there weren't any ranch guests milling around in the dark.

Deacon took another swig from the bottle and wiped his mouth. He hadn't been one-hundred-percent honest with Ray. He had been in love with RJ once upon a time, but his friend had shut him down. He now knew the reason. At the time, RJ had confided in Deacon that he loved him like a son, now Deacon knew why. RJ had been mourning for the son he'd never been allowed to get to know.

What would RJ think if he knew how badly Deacon wanted to bury his cock in Ray's ass? He snorted. It went beyond sex and he knew it. There was something about Ray that called up all Deacon's protective instincts. He wanted to hold the smaller man and never let him go.

He wandered into the living room to his small desk in the corner. Pulling out the top drawer, he lifted the envelope with his name on it. Mr. Krueger had given Deacon an envelope earlier in the week, with a message from RJ not to open it until he had befriended Ray. Deacon supposed seducing his best friend's son wasn't quite what RJ had had in mind.

Deacon still wasn't sure what the hell that was supposed to mean. What could RJ have possibly wanted to tell Deacon that he hadn't already told him?

After another tip of the bottle, Deacon took the letter over to the couch. He set the whiskey on the coffee table and opened the letter.

Chapter Three

Dressed in a pair of black slacks and a white shirt, Ray fingered the turquoise slide attached to the bolo tie he'd found on his dad's dresser. The silver on the tips and of the braded piece of leather appeared old and worn. Ray had no doubt it had been one of his father's favorites. He hoped no one minded him wearing it.

He was surprised to find Dandy already saddled and waiting outside the barn. "Hey, girl." He smoothed his hand down the horse's ginger-colored coat. A shadow fell over him and Ray turned, expecting to see Deacon.

"Oh, hi, Cody."

The young, good-looking cowboy tipped his hat. "I figured you'd be riding Dandy. I hope you don't mind me getting her ready for you."

"Not at all. Thanks." Ray glanced around. "Is Deacon with the guests?"

"Naw. He talked to them yesterday when they came in. He explained about RJ's death and they agreed to lie low this morning until after the services."

"Oh. That's good." He slid his borrowed pair of boots around in the dirt. "Do you know where Deacon is?"

Cody shook his head. "Haven't seen him yet, but we all figured he needed some time alone, so no one's gone looking."

Ray returned his attention to his horse. He remembered Deacon telling him he had stuff to do, but he'd hoped... Oh hell, he didn't know what he hoped.

"Feel like eating some breakfast?" Cody asked.

"Sure." Ray gave Dandy another scratch under her forelock and followed Cody across the road. The large passenger van used to ferry guests around sat in front of the cookhouse. "How many people are expected?"

Cody glanced up the ranch road. "Hard to say, but I figure around fifty riders, maybe another six or seven in the van. The trailers should be pulling in any time."

Ray noticed Cody's continual glances at his borrowed tie. "Is it okay that I wore this?"

Cody nodded. "Sure. RJ always wore it to greet guests and on the nights when he and Deacon would make the big supper for the guests in the old summer cabin."

Ray hated to admit it, but he'd not yet been inside the large log structure everyone called the summer cabin. "I've been meaning to get up there, but now it's full of guests."

"Not all of it. The guests stay in the newer side. The original side, the one built by your great-great-grandfather, is used primarily for the once-a-week guest dinners and that's where we always have had our Thanksgiving and Christmas dinners. RJ had the kitchen redone a couple years ago. It's a chef's delight, according to Deacon."

"You guys stick around for the holidays?" Ray picked up a plate and began filling it with scrambled eggs and bacon.

Before answering, Cody glanced around the room. Most of the people had already eaten, Ray could tell by the crumbs on the red-and-white-checked tablecloths. Cody looked sideways at Ray and lowered his voice. "Most of us are here because we're not really welcome at our folks' houses."

Puzzled by the statement, Ray carried his plate to the table. Once Cody was across from him, he leaned in. "Would it be rude if I asked why you weren't welcome?"

Cody reached for a biscuit. He split it in two and slathered it with fresh butter. "Mostly the gay thing, but we don't really advertise that to the guests, so keep it under your hat."

Ray stopped with a forkful of eggs halfway to his mouth. "You're all gay?"

Cody chuckled. "You didn't know?"

Ray shook his head.

"Years ago, after Deacon got beat up so bad by those boys from the outfit he used to work for, RJ went up north and fetched him from the hospital. He brought him here to the J Bar and told him he could be himself here. Word kinda got around and here we are. All misfits, according to the rugged cowboys of Montana, Texas and Wyoming."

Ray stuck the food in his mouth. "But the guests don't know? How is that being yourself?"

With his red eyebrows drawn together, Cody jabbed at the eggs on his plate with his fork. "Just because we're not allowed to flaunt our sexuality in front of the guests doesn't mean we're not allowed to be ourselves. You're gay, right?"

"Yeah."

"Do you walk around talking about other men and stuff at your job back home?" Cody asked.

Ray shook his head. "I get your point."

* * * * *

Deacon stumbled to the kitchen and fixed a pot of coffee. It felt like a brass band was having a jam session in his head. He leaned over and dug RJ's wadded-up letter out of the trash.

He set it on the counter and tried to smooth out some of the wrinkles from his tantrum the previous night. When he'd thrown it away he had no intentions of reading the vile thing again, but he'd woke up realizing maybe it was the alcohol that had been the trouble and not the words written on the page.

Without waiting for the pot to finish, Deacon stuck his cup under the automatic drip. It would be stronger than hell, but the way he felt, he needed it. Taking his coffee and the letter back to the table, he pulled out a chair and sat down.

He read through RJ's letter and cursed once again. Even semi-sober, the words written on the page were in stark contradiction to the man he'd known.

My Dear Old Friend,

If you're reading this it means you've struck up some sort of friendship with my wayward son. Please don't be fooled by him. He's as conniving as they come and will think nothing of selling off the land my family has spent years acquiring.

Ray's words came back to him. His new friend had been right, RJ did think of his son as a spoiled brat.

Deacon skipped the part where RJ confessed to initially breaking all ties to his ex-wife and son. He didn't feel like reading his old friend whine about how he married when he was too young and afraid to come out of the closet. Deacon didn't even care that RJ had a brief affair with a male coworker that led to the breakup of his marriage. He'd left his wife and son behind to pursue his "true self" as RJ had called it. Deacon called it pure selfishness.

It was no wonder after a couple of years and a few more failed relationships, RJ started to feel guilty about the way he'd left Ray Jr. When he'd received the letter from Ray's mom telling him Ray had no desire to see or speak to him, RJ had all but given up. RJ still followed Ray Jr.'s life and paid for his school, but the bitterness he felt toward his only son ate at him like a cancer.

Deacon's attention went back to RJ's written words.

When I found out my heart was giving out, I hired a private detective. I needed to know exactly what type of man my only heir had become. The report I received back made me even angrier. How dare Ray Jr. spit at a relationship with me when he himself is gay?

Believe me, Deacon, if I could leave you the ranch, I would. Unfortunately, a provision of my great-grandfather's will doesn't leave me that choice. Either the ranch goes to my direct descendant or it is to be sold. We both know I can't allow that. This is where I'm going to ask you the biggest favor of my life.

I need you to seduce my son. I'm not asking you to fall in love with him, but I need Ray Jr. to think you have. Use every skill you have as a lover to convince him not to sell the Justice ranch. I'm begging you. In the end, I hope you break his heart. I only wish I could be there to see the anguish in Ray Jr.'s face. Let him know what it feels like to love someone who doesn't love you back. It would be the perfect revenge for me, my friend.

Deacon dropped the letter, disgusted once again. He'd been so worried about following his instincts with Ray because of his friendship with RJ. Come to find out, he was playing into RJ's plan without even knowing it.

Deacon pushed himself away from the table and went back to bed. "Fuck RJ and his funeral."

As he lay down and covered himself, thoughts of Ray continued to plague him. Now he knew the circumstances behind Ray and RJ's relationship, or lack thereof, he felt even worse for the younger man.

Images of Ray riding up the ridge to pay tribute to a man who was capable of such subterfuge hurt. With a groan, Deacon threw the covers back and climbed out of bed.

* * * * *

Deacon could see the slow-moving procession make its way toward the ridge as he led Black Jack out of the barn. He didn't know who'd saddled his horse, but he'd be forever grateful. He swung himself into the soft leather saddle and took off at a run toward Ray.

Within minutes he could see Ray's slumped shoulders as he rode just behind the buckboard wagon carrying his father. In that moment, Deacon vowed to do what was best for Ray regardless of what RJ wanted. He still didn't understand his friend's reasoning, but he also refused to live the rest of his life wondering. He was glad he'd burned the letter. He hoped no one, especially Ray, ever found out just what RJ thought of his son.

Ray must have heard him coming because he pulled Dandy to a stop and glanced over his shoulder. Deacon knew the smile the solemn man gave him was worth risking everything for.

He stopped Black Jack beside Dandy. Without a word, he leaned across the distance and gave Ray a deep but short kiss. "I'm sorry I wasn't here."

Ray licked his lips. "I was afraid you weren't coming because of what happened last night."

Deacon shook his head. "What happened between us is the reason I came at all."

Ray's black eyebrows drew together. "I don't understand."

The last thing he'd ever do was purposely hurt Ray, so telling the younger man about the letter wasn't an option. "Doesn't matter. Let's go say goodbye to RJ."

Deacon could tell Ray still didn't understand Deacon's conflicting moods, but he eventually nodded. They caught up to the buckboard, riding side by side as the wagon crested the top of the ridge on the narrow and rutted dirt path.

Because it was expected, Deacon helped the other cowboys carry the simple coffin to the pre-dug hole. They lowered it the old-fashioned way, with ropes cradling the bottom and sides. Once RJ was in his final resting place, Deacon stepped back and took his place at Ray's side.

As he listened to Reverend Peters speak of all the good things RJ had accomplished in his life for the people of Montana, a pain started in Deacon's chest. He knew everything the reverend said was correct. RJ had done all those things. What he was struggling with was his new protective instincts toward Ray.

He reached for Ray's hand as Reverend Peters finished out the service. It was customary to eulogize the deceased, but

RJ had always hated the custom, so Deacon had decided to do away with it. Given the circumstances, he was glad he had. He knew it was hurt clouding his judgment and hopefully, in time, the good memories of the man everyone was standing around crying over would come back.

Ray squeezed his hand, drawing Deacon's attention. He gazed down at the smaller man and gave Ray a reassuring smile. Ray's green eyes were watery but he wasn't crying.

"Feel like going for a short ride with me?" Deacon asked as Jimmy and Neil began filling the grave with dirt.

Ray glanced around at the mourners and nodded. "I'd like that. I feel like everyone's staring at me."

Deacon drew Ray away from the crowd. "It's not you. It's the resemblance to your father."

After thanking the reverend, they walked to their tethered horses. Deacon sat proud as Ray mounted Dandy on his own. "Gettin' better," he remarked.

Ray grinned. "I think it's the pants. They're not as tight as my jeans."

"I like your jeans, so if it means I need to lift you into the saddle to get you to wear them, I'm all for it."

Ray had an odd expression on his face as they started to ride down toward Logan's Landing. "What's going on?"

"What do you mean?" Deacon asked.

"Did the ghost of Christmas Past visit you last night? Because when you left after that brief kiss, I thought you'd decided I wasn't worth your time."

"No. I never felt it wasn't worth my time. I was just worried about RJ and how he would've felt about it." Deacon shook his head. "I've decided I don't care. I like you."

Ray grinned. "I like you, too."

Deacon rode toward a spot he wanted to show Ray. "There's a bend up here in the river that the locals have named after your family."

"Seriously? I have a bend?" Ray chuckled. "That's way better than my parking spot back home."

Deacon chuckled and shook his head as they arrived at the bend. "You're in an awfully good mood for a man who just attended a funeral."

He regretted the quip as soon as it left his mouth. Ray's expression clouded. "You're right. I'm sorry."

Deacon pulled Black Jack to a stop and dismounted. He wound his horse's reins around a small tree branch and did the same to Dandy before helping Ray down from RJ's saddle.

"That was a thoughtless thing for me to say. I should be the one apologizing." Deacon crushed his mouth against Ray's with all the passion he'd held inside since meeting the man. He swept his tongue through the interior of Ray's mouth and moaned when he felt his soon-to-be lover reciprocate.

The kiss went deeper, more carnal than anything Deacon had experienced in a long time. His hands slid down Ray's back to squeeze that cute little ass he'd been watching for days.

Deacon thrust his leg between Ray's thighs and lifted him slightly off the ground. Ray broke the kiss and gazed up into Deacon's eyes as he began to grind against him.

"I want you," Ray gasped, rubbing his hard cock against Deacon's thigh.

"You've got me." Deacon knew he was lost the moment he'd brushed his lips across Ray's the previous evening.

He felt Ray's hands at the slide fastening of his dress slacks. "I don't have anything with me."

Ray smiled and slid Deacon's zipper down over his prominent bulge. "We'll save the fucking for a bed, but I want to taste you."

Deacon didn't normally engage in oral sex without the protection of a condom, but Ray wasn't some stranger he'd met in a bar. He nodded his consent as Ray slid to the ground at Deacon's feet.

With his knees already weak, Deacon glanced around. "Hang on." He scooped Ray up in his arms and started to carry him toward a tree. "Shit. Hold my pants up, will ya?"

Laughing, Ray reached between them and did as asked. "Wouldn't want you to trip and fall on a thornbush with your junk all exposed."

Deacon chuckled. He found a soft grassy area under a large tree and set Ray down. With his back braced against the trunk of a cottonwood, Deacon guided Ray's mouth to his cock.

The first swipe of Ray's tongue across the crown of his shaft made Deacon shudder with pleasure and bury his fingers in the man's black hair. "Yes, lick it."

Ray went to work on Deacon's cock, licking it from tip to root, following the thick veins with his tongue. Never had he been so grateful for a mouth in his life. "Jesus! You're gonna kill me."

Ray answered by tickling Deacon's balls with a flick of his tongue. The torture had gone on long enough, in Deacon's mind. He reached down and pointed the head of his cock toward Ray's mouth. "Please?"

Ray nodded and spit into the palm of his hand. He wrapped the lubricated hand around the base of Deacon's cock as he stuffed as much of Deacon's length as he could down his throat.

"Fuck!" With every suck Ray bestowed, Deacon felt a jolt of electricity run up his spine. He tilted his head back and stared up through the leaves of the tree. As he felt the continual pull to his cock, he began to wonder what the tree would look like from the exact same vantage point the other three seasons of the year. He smiled at the thought of trekking through the snow to receive a winter blowjob from the man currently doing a fantastic job of deep throating his entire length.

Ray stabbed his tongue into the slit on top of Deacon's crown, sending Deacon's lust into overdrive. He couldn't help himself. He began a slow thrust in and out of Ray's mouth. Deacon's jaws clenched as he tried to stave off his imminent climax. *Two more minutes, please, God, two more minutes,* he repeated over and over to himself as Ray did the swirly thing with his tongue again. It didn't take long for his balls to draw up tight. Deacon's teeth were damn near ground to powder as he fought to hold off. When his cock was once again swallowed to the root, Deacon knew he'd reached his limit. "Gonna shoot."

Ray's mouth backed off, but continued to jack Deacon's cock with his hand. Deacon growled as the first rope of cum landed on Ray's cheek. Deacon stared down as he painted the gorgeous man with four more strands of thick white fluid.

Deacon fell to his knees and bathed his lover's face with his tongue, enjoying his own seed mixed with Ray's salty skin. Ray turned his head and found Deacon's mouth, licking at the interior.

Once his lover was thoroughly cleaned, Deacon sat back and stared into those brilliant green eyes. "Your turn."

Ray chuckled and lifted his hand. Deacon had been so into the expert blowjob, he hadn't even realized Ray had been jacking himself off at the same time. He grabbed Ray's hand and slowly licked it clean, sucking the younger man's long, elegant fingers into his mouth one at a time.

"Fuck, that's hot," Ray rasped.

Deacon lay in the soft grass and pulled Ray into his arms. He pointed toward the water. "That's Justice River. It's actually a tributary of the Yellowstone River, but Justice River is what everyone around here knows it by. It's been a godsend on more than one occasion. The other creeks on the J Bar have been known to dry up during bad summers, but the Justice River never has. It's the lifeblood of this ranch and the bordering ranches."

Ray rested his cheek on Deacon's chest. "There's so much of my family's history here. It's a shame I don't know more about it."

"There are a couple of journals in the summer cabin written by your great-grandfather. Nothing life altering, but he does talk about the everyday happenings here on the ranch."

"You'll have to show me. I still haven't even been inside the summer cabin. Where'd the name come from?"

"Your dad. He nicknamed it that when we started allowing guests to stay there. Other than the fireplaces, the heating sucks. It was all added about twenty years ago. They couldn't put central heating in because it would ruin the log cabin's aesthetic value, so it's all baseboard heat. It's the reason we don't have guests in the winter."

They lay in silence for a while before Ray groaned. "We should probably get back to the dinner. I'd also like to spend some time with the guests later."

"You would?"

"Sure. I have a few big decisions in front of me. I'd like to talk to the guests and see what they do and don't like about the ranch. I'd also like to spend some time with Beth going over the books."

Deacon was taken aback. "I'm surprised you've given this so much thought already."

Ray smiled up at him. "Don't be. I'm not only a creative genius, but I've got a damn good head for business."

Deacon knew from long evenings with RJ that the ranch barely managed to stay in the black most years. He wondered if Ray would decide taking a big cash payment from the developers would be the better business decision. His thoughts returned to RJ's letter. No matter what Ray decided to do with the ranch, Deacon knew he couldn't use his personal feelings for Ray against him. Trying to sway the new owner one way or the other wasn't going to happen.

* * * * *

By the time they rode back to the barn, Ray could tell the majority of the mourners had gone. He glanced at Deacon. "Think people are mad we didn't show up?"

Deacon shook his head. "Naw. People are pretty easygoing around here. They probably figured we needed some time."

Ray dismounted Dandy and rubbed his sore ass. He wasn't sure what hurt more, his ass or his inner thighs. "I think I need to give the saddle a break for a day or two."

Deacon chuckled as he started unsaddling Dandy. "You just need to work your way up to the longer rides. You'll get used to it."

Neil pulled up beside them in one of the ranch pickups. He had several guests in the back along with some sacks and big white squares. "I'm heading out to Cottman's Valley to put out minerals and salt blocks," he told Deacon.

Deacon nodded and Neil started to drive off.

"Wait!" Ray called. "You mind if I tag along?"

Neil seemed surprised at the request. "Not at all." Neil said something to the man sitting in the cab with him and the man got out and climbed into the bed of the truck.

"You don't have to do that. I can ride in the back." Even though Ray knew the other cowboys thought he was a prissy city boy, he wanted so badly to fit in on the ranch.

The older man waved his hand. "Don't worry about it. I'll be perfectly comfortable back here. I just didn't want Neil to ride alone up there."

Ray could tell the guest was just being nice, but he nodded his acceptance of the gesture. "Thanks."

He turned back to Deacon. "Catch up with you later?"

"You'd better or else I'll have to hunt you down."

Ray got in the truck and buckled his seat belt. "I hope you don't mind me coming along."

"Not at all. I usually do this with the guests a couple times a week. It gets them off their horses for a bit and allows them to see more of the ranch," Neil explained.

Ray chuckled and dramatically rubbed his sore backside. "I understand the need of getting a break from the horses."

Neil pulled out onto the ranch road and headed west. Ray took several sideways glances at the man, trying to determine if Neil was also gay. The rugged-looking cowboy didn't set off his gaydar, but then again, not one cowboy had.

Neil started to smile. "Yes."

"Huh?"

"You were wondering about my sexuality, right? The answer to your unspoken question is yes."

Ray scratched the back of his neck. "Was I being that obvious?"

Neil chuckled. "Not really, but Cody told me the two of you had talked about it. Let me put your mind at ease. We're all pretty much gay except the cooks. Beth has a male partner she lives with in Roscoe. Until recently, I had a fella I used to occasionally see in Billings."

Ray sat back in the seat and stared out his window. With a ranch full of gay men, he began to wonder about other things. "Do you ever have gay guests?"

Neil's eyebrows shot up as he squirmed in his seat. "Once in a while."

"Anything ever happen between a guest and someone on staff?"

Neil shook his head. "It's not that we haven't been tempted a time or two, but we've usually got families staying with us."

Ray nodded. He wondered if there was an untapped market staring him in the face. The J Bar was unique, no two ways about it. Maybe they should consider opening the ranch up to special groups. It was definitely something he'd bring up to Deacon later.

Chapter Four

ಸಿ

Deacon didn't see Ray again until he arrived at the cookhouse for supper that night. He did his best to mingle with the guests before filling his plate and sitting next to his new lover. "Did ya have a productive day?"

Ray grinned and nudged Deacon with his knee. "A very productive day. How about you?"

Deacon chuckled and sopped some of his gravy up with a piece of homemade bread. "It had its moments."

"Hey, Deacon," Taggert said from the doorway. "Lambert just called and said he's got some of our cattle on his side of the fence."

"Shit. Okay. Eat up and we'll ride out." He turned to Cody. "You'll have to start the campfire without us."

"Yes, boss."

Deacon knocked elbows with Ray. "You up to a ride, or would you rather sing songs and tell stories with the guests?"

Ray finished his bite of salad. "How far is it?"

Deacon grinned. He knew Ray's ass was probably sore, so it was more a test than anything. "Only about a thirty-minute ride, but across some pretty rough ground."

Staring down into his chicken and dumplings, Ray licked his lips. "What do you think I should do?"

"Let me think on it for a few minutes." The more Deacon considered his options, the clearer his decision became. Unfortunately, the middle of the dining room wasn't the place to discuss them with Ray.

He quickly finished his dinner and took his plate up and put it in the wash bucket before sneaking into the kitchen to give Martha a kiss on the cheek. "Great dinner, Mother."

Martha patted Deacon's cheek. "You gettin' sweet on that boy in there?"

Deacon followed Mother's gaze to Ray, who was scraping his leftovers in the chicken feed bucket. "He's not a boy, but he sure as hell is pretty, isn't he?"

Martha chuckled. "You always did have an eye for the pretty ones."

"Beats the alternative," he said, poking Martha in the side before scurrying out of the kitchen.

He caught up with Ray on the front porch. "So?" Ray asked. "Am I going?"

Deacon led Ray off the porch and to the barn. Once inside, he cornered his lover in the tack room and pressed their bodies together. "Here's what I'm thinking. If you ride with me over to Lambert's, you won't feel like riding me after the campfire."

He leaned in and ran his tongue across Ray's cheek to delve deep into his mouth. His fingers found their way into the black spiky hair as the kiss went into overdrive. Only when he was in dire need of oxygen did he break away. "Feel like singing happy songs with the guests before letting me pile drive this sweet ass?"

"Oh yeah. I can play nice with an incentive like that."

Deacon heard the other cowhands entering the barn. He gave Ray one last kiss and swatted his butt. "You take good care of this now and I'll reward you for it later."

Chuckling, Ray shook his head and cupped Deacon's cock in his hand. "Ditto."

* * * * *

Ray actually felt nervous as he joined Cody and about sixteen guests in the large front yard of the summer cabin. It was his first ever campfire and Lord knew he didn't know a single cowboy song.

He found an empty spot on one of the large smooth logs. "May I sit by you?"

The older mother of two smiled. "Sure. As long as you do me a favor and laugh at my jokes. It'll be good for Jeff to catch a little of the green-eyed monster."

Ray chuckled and settled in beside the woman. "I'm Ray, by the way."

"Jennifer." She pointed down the log beside her. "That's my daughter Bethanne, my son David and my husband of eighteen years, Jeff. Are you married?"

Ray shook his head. "I'm gay."

He caught a surprised expression on Cody's face as the cowboy walked in front of Ray and sat beside him. Jennifer smiled and patted Ray's knee. "Well, have you found a nice young man then?"

"I'm working on it."

* * * * *

After more songs than he cared to think about, Ray received an elbow to the side.

"Mind helping me get the stuff for s'mores?" Cody asked.

"Not at all." Ray jumped at the chance to escape the noise for a few moments. He followed Cody into the older wing of the summer cabin and into the brightly lit gourmet kitchen. "Damn."

Cody chuckled. "Doesn't quite fit in with the rest of the place, does it?"

Ray ran his hand over the light-colored granite countertop. He could feel Cody's eyes on him and glanced up. "What?"

Cody took off his hat and ran his fingers through his short auburn hair. "We're not really supposed to let the guests know we're gay."

"What? She asked. I didn't just volunteer the information."

Cody nodded. "I know."

Ray narrowed his eyes. "Is this one of Deacon's rules or was it my father's?"

Cody turned and started loading a tray with graham crackers, marshmallows and chocolate bars. "Your dad's."

Ray wanted to tell Cody to forget about the fucked-up rule, but he knew he'd better discuss it with Deacon first. Maybe there was a reason for the stupid rule he wasn't aware of. "I'll talk to Deacon about it."

Cody nodded. "I just thought I'd mention it." Cody held out the tray. "If you'll take this out, I'll get the cider."

Ray carried the goodies outside and set them on the picnic table. He was more than pleased to see Deacon and the rest of the ranch hands back. He caught Deacon's eye and waved.

Although Deacon was talking to one of the guests, he excused himself and walked over. "Having fun?"

Ray smiled. "It would help if I knew some of the songs. Here," he said, holding out the tray, "make yourself useful. I've never made a s'more in my life."

Deacon gave a playful gasp. "Bite your tongue. S'mores are the heaven of all cowboys."

"Really?" He leaned in to whisper in Deacon's ear. "And here I thought sex was."

Deacon chuckled. "That, too. But eating melting chocolatey goodness is something we can do in public."

Deacon walked off and Ray glanced toward the fire. He watched as the couple he'd sat with earlier leaned toward each other for a kiss. *Why can't I do that?* He sighed and sat on one of the logs while Deacon and a few of the hands helped the guests with their dessert.

In the red and orange glow of the firelight, he studied Deacon with the ranch hands and guests. Although Deacon was polite, there seemed to be something missing. It was almost like Deacon had erected a wall between himself and the guests. Ray wondered if it had anything to do with the need to hide who he was.

Ray had witnessed Deacon working side by side with the ranch hands and he seemed easier, happier. He wanted to see that side of Deacon all the time, not just when he wasn't around guests.

The wheels started turning. He'd already had a chance to sit down and go over the books with Beth earlier in the afternoon. Summers were a big time for the ranch, but the guest side of the business wasn't as good in the spring and fall. Beth had explained school played a large part in that. Families tended to come during summer break. It was just something RJ had always planned on and worked around.

Ray might not be a lot of help moving cattle and helping with the everyday chores, but he knew how to market and advertise. Perhaps a new strategy would make the J Bar bigger than it had ever been. He wasn't completely oblivious to his own motives. Although he'd never been given the chance before, it was something Ray could do in the names of the men who'd lived and worked the ranch for generations.

Ray decided not to get Deacon or anyone else's hopes up until he'd done his research. He would have his work cut out for him if he was going to finish before he hopped a plane in five days, but if everything worked out, it would give him a reason to come back.

* * * * *

By eleven o'clock, Deacon had had all the smiling he could stand for one day. He said his goodnights to the guests and tipped his hat toward Ray, hoping his new lover would understand the signal.

He started down the washed-out dirt path and waited for Ray to join him. He heard running feet behind him and turned in time to see Ray skidding to a stop.

"What the fuck was that about?" Ray asked, his eyebrows drawn together. "For two hours I sat there waiting for you to be ready to go and then you just left me."

Deacon shook his head. "What do you think I tipped my hat for? I wanted you to make your excuses and follow me."

"So why didn't you just say, 'Hey, let's go'?"

Deacon couldn't figure out why Ray seemed so bent out of shape. He gestured to the few remaining guests. "You don't think anyone would've thought it strange that we're walking off together?"

Ray reached up and began tugging on his hair. "I can't fucking stand this anymore."

Without saying anything else, Ray ran toward the main house.

Deacon was left wondering what the hell had just happened. He took off his hat and slapped it against his thigh. It seemed Ray still wasn't used to the way things worked on ranches and in small towns around the country.

He continued walking until he came to the fork in the road, one way led to the main house, the other to his own cottage. Did he go after Ray or let the younger man cool down? He knew the day had been hard on Ray. Maybe it was the culmination of grief and stress that was getting to him.

Settling his hat back on his head, Deacon headed up the driveway toward Ray's. It was one of the only graveled roads on the ranch and he found it uncomfortable to walk on. He veered toward the side and was soon walking in the grass. He crossed the yard and took the porch steps two at a time.

Deacon lifted his hand to knock when movement out of the corner of his eye caught his attention. He turned to find

Ray sitting in one of the chairs at the corner of the wide front porch.

He took several steps and leaned his hip against the porch rail. "You still pissed?"

"I like you."

Although it was too dark to see Ray's face, Deacon got the feeling the man wasn't too happy about the admission.

"I like you, too," he answered.

"Really? So why are you so afraid to show it?"

Instead of answering right away, Deacon moved to sit in one of the chairs opposite Ray. "You never know how straight folks will react. Bottom line is that I've learned to hide myself around them."

"What kind of life is that?"

Deacon tossed his hat to the small table beside him. "Beats the hell out of dying. Which I almost did before I came here." Deacon sighed and decided to tell Ray something very few people knew. "Remember I told you I worked on a ranch up north? Well, one of the cowboys I shared a room with found a picture I'd torn out of a magazine. I had it good and hid, but he'd been snooping in my shit."

Deacon scrubbed his hands together. It didn't matter how many years he put behind him, the incident would forever remain in the forefront. "Men I thought were my friends conspired behind my back. They dragged me out of my bunk one night and tied me to a tree. They took turns throwing punches and by the time they were finished, I was near dead. If it hadn't been for the ranch owner coming out to see what all the commotion was about, I've no doubt I would've died that night."

He heard Ray's indrawn breath.

"You may think I'm a coward, but I'm alive and doing the job I was born to do."

Ray got to his feet and came to stand in front of Deacon. "This is your home, though."

Deacon reached out and pulled Ray onto his lap. "Yeah. It is. The only one I've ever had that accepted who I am."

Ray cupped Deacon's cheek and kissed his forehead. "If it's time for confessions, I guess you've earned the right to hear mine. Until a few minutes ago, I was beginning to think I could settle here. I know it would be a huge adjustment, but I see the way you and the other hands are together."

Deacon could see tears reflecting in Ray's green depths by the light of the moon as his lover continued.

"I want that. I want a group of friends I can joke with, have fun with. People who'll have my back when times get hard."

"You can have it, all of it," Deacon told him.

Ray shook his head. "Not if I have to hide who I truly am every time we get another van full of guests. My father gave all of you a safe place to live and work. It was my understanding that being gay was acceptable on the J Bar, but little did I know, it was only accepted behind closed doors. I can't live like that. I won't."

"What're you saying?" Deacon felt like his heart was being ripped from his chest. He'd known Ray only a short while, but it was the first time in his life he'd met someone he could see himself feeling complete with.

Ray rested his forehead against Deacon's. "I'm saying I can't allow myself to fall in love with you under those circumstances."

Ray started to pull away, but Deacon's arms tightened, holding him in place. He wasn't sure what to say to the man, but Deacon knew he couldn't let Ray walk away. "Under what circumstances *can* you see yourself falling in love with me?"

Ray placed a soft, gentle kiss on Deacon's mouth. "One where I can do *that* if I want to. I sat there tonight and watched other couples holding hands and sneaking kisses. I want that.

My feelings for you are no less because we're both men and if people can't understand that, I'm not sure I should welcome them into my home and on my land."

"We need the business. It's not as easy nowadays to make a go of a ranch this size. The revenue from the guests keeps us afloat."

"Then maybe we need to look into getting a different type of guest. Perhaps people who're accepting of alternative lifestyles."

Deacon had a strong feeling he knew where Ray was going, but he had serious doubts. He shook his head. "We won't be able to find enough..."

Ray kissed him again. "The world's full of gay men. Leave it to me to find them and bring them here."

"Like a gay man's version of *Field of Dreams*?"

Ray laughed. "Yeah, something like that. But seriously...think about it. How many times have you been able to go on vacation with a lover and felt totally free to put your arm around him or kiss him if the mood was right?"

Deacon had never been on a real vacation, let alone done anything remotely like what Ray was talking about. "So you really want to make the J Bar a vacation spot for gay men?"

"Not just that, but alternative families, lesbians, hell, I'm not picky as long as the guests who come don't mind seeing me kiss you once in a while. I was going over the books with Beth and it looks like spring and fall are hard times here on the ranch. Maybe we can reserve those seasons for the GLBT guests and then take it from there?"

Deacon wasn't sure it would work, but he really liked the thought of Ray staying. If it took revamping the ranch, so be it. "You'd have to move here."

Ray rubbed his nose across Deacon's. "Well, I wouldn't *have* to move here, but I'd probably want to. Marketing is done primarily over the computer, so wherever I have access to the internet would work."

"The ranch office has internet, so does RJ's."

"So you think it's a good idea?" Ray asked.

At that point, Deacon didn't care if the idea flopped. The important thing was spending time with Ray. "I think we should go for it."

Ray kissed him, flicking the tip of his tongue against Deacon's. "How about we go upstairs and celebrate?"

Deacon squeezed Ray's ass. "I've thought of nothing else since I met you."

Ray climbed off Deacon's lap and held out his hand, pulling Deacon to his feet. Deacon led the way, surprised when he couldn't get in. "You locked the door?"

Ray dug the keys out of his pocket and handed them to Deacon. "Of course I locked it. Why wouldn't I?"

Deacon tended to forget Ray wasn't from the country. He fit the key into the deadbolt and opened the house before handing them back to Ray. "With the exception of the office, we don't lock doors around here. We've never once had a problem with leaving our houses open."

Ray went inside and tossed the keys on the entry table. "That'll take some getting used to. At home I wouldn't even take out the garbage without locking up behind me."

Deacon put a hand to Ray's back and led him to the stairs. "This is your home now, so show a little trust."

Ray turned around and began walking up the steps backward. He unbuttoned his shirt and let it fall from his shoulders.

Deacon couldn't resist and ran his hand down Ray's smooth chest to the light treasure trail just under his bellybutton. "You are so damn sexy."

Ray's smile lit up his entire face as he popped the button on his jeans. "And that's not even my best feature."

With Ray standing on the step above him, it put them nose to nose. Deacon reached out and grabbed the back of

Ray's neck, pulling his lover in for a kiss. As his tongue tangled with Ray's, he unzipped the smaller man's jeans and pushed them down as far as he could.

Deacon broke the kiss and grinned. "Sit."

Ray bit his plump lower lip as he sat down and kicked his jeans and underwear off. He spread his thighs and leaned his arms back on the step above him. "Is this what you had in mind?"

Deacon knelt and braced his hands on the same step Ray's feet rested on. He was finished talking. All he could think about was the cock in front of him, dripping with pre-come.

He started at Ray's firm sac and worked his way up the long, thin length, stopping occasionally to scrape the flesh with his teeth.

Ray moaned as he reached out with one hand to grab a fistful of Deacon's hair. "More."

Deacon knew there was no need for Ray to beg. He hadn't even tasted his prize yet, no way was he going to quit. He ran his tongue around the ridge of the crown, lapping the pre-come as it continued to drip from the slit at the top.

"Mmmm." He hummed as he slipped his lips over the head, Ray's taste exploding in his mouth.

Ray's grip on Deacon's hair tightened as he thrust his hips, driving his cock deeper down Deacon's throat.

Deacon put a hand on Ray's stomach, holding him back as he released the cock in his mouth. He couldn't believe he was about to ruin the unbelievably erotic moment. "Sorry, but my knees are killing me. Guess I'm not as young as I used to be."

Ray chuckled and moved up a step so he could stand without sending Deacon tumbling down the stairs. "Come on, old man. I'll help you to bed."

Deacon happily followed Ray's nude body. Hell, at that point, he was afraid he'd follow Ray anywhere he wanted to lead. He was surprised when Ray bypassed the master bedroom.

Deacon had been in RJ's room on many occasions, but never in the capacity of lover. "Why aren't you in the big bedroom?"

Ray glanced over his shoulder. "It's not mine. I can't sleep in the same bed my father fucked his lovers."

Deacon chuckled. "You have an inflated view of RJ's sex life. He never brought a man home."

Ray spun around, a shocked expression on his face. "He never had sex?"

"I didn't say that. He'd go into Billings one weekend a month."

"What is it with Billings? Neil said that's where he went, too." A thought struck him. "Were my dad and Neil lovers?"

Deacon shrugged. "If they were, no one told me about it. Billings is the only place around with a gay bar. Hell, there are only like four in the entire state. If a guy wants to meet a like-minded man, he goes to The Loft."

Ray entered one of the spare rooms and climbed into an unmade bed. "Enough talking, more getting naked."

Deacon pulled the front of his shirt and the pearl snaps gave way.

"Slower," Ray admonished. "I want to see every inch of your body."

Deacon chuckled. "I'm a cowboy, not a stripper."

He sat on the bed and pulled off his boots and socks before standing to face Ray. His lover was lounging on a pile of pillows propped against the headboard. "Besides, I've waited long enough."

A thought suddenly struck him. "You got stuff?"

Ray scurried off the bed and disappeared into the bathroom. Deacon finished undressing and lay down. He ran his hands over his body, settling one on his chest while the other began to stroke his erection.

When Ray didn't come back right away, Deacon called out. "You fall in?"

"No. Just give me a sec."

Deacon noted something different in Ray's voice and curiosity got the better of him. He hopped out of bed and went to investigate. The sight that met him nearly made him shoot right then and there.

With one foot resting on the toilet, Ray was inserting a rather large dildo up his ass. With Ray's back to him, Deacon had the perfect view of the flesh-colored silicone as it slid its way home. "I thought that was my job."

Ray jumped and looked over his shoulder. His face was red from apparent embarrassment, but Deacon could detect the flush of arousal as well. "I like to stretch myself beforehand."

Different. Deacon stepped forward and nudged the dildo with his hand. "So, me doing this is off-limits?"

Ray gasped and Deacon took control of the toy. He began twisting it as he pumped the rigid silicone in and out of Ray's hole. As Deacon watched his lover's body respond to the fake cock, he couldn't help but imagine his own shaft stabbing into Ray's depths.

He leaned in and sucked Ray's earlobe, pushing the dildo in as far as it would go. "Why do you do this before you fuck?"

Ray's back arched as he moaned. "Sometimes it hurts in the beginning. I didn't want that. Especially not with you."

Before Deacon could move the dildo again, Ray began rocking his hips, fucking himself. "Damn, babe. I can't stand it. I want to feel you. Make you fly."

Deacon removed the dildo and tossed it into the sink. He replaced the artificial cock with his finger. Despite having just been fucked by a piece of silicone, Deacon couldn't get over the squeeze of Ray's inner walls. "You're small, tight." He didn't want to brag, but Deacon knew his cock was bigger than the toy Ray had been used to using. "Promise me something?"

"Anything," Ray said around a moan.

"If I start hurting you, make sure you tell me."

Ray nodded, as he rode Deacon's fingers.

Satisfied, Deacon glanced around and spotted Ray's shaving kit on the back of the toilet. "Grab the stuff and let me take you to bed."

Ray reached into the black leather bag and pulled out a strip of condoms and a small tube of lubricant. Deacon lifted his lover into his arms and carried him to bed. He could feel the pre-come dripping down his shaft as he walked across the room and carefully deposited Ray on the big mattress.

Deacon positioned himself between Ray's spread thighs and opened one of the packages. He rolled the condom down his length and applied more lube to his cock and Ray's stretched hole.

"Remember what I asked," he reminded Ray as he positioned the crown of his cock at the smaller man's entrance.

Deacon's jaws clenched as he tried to enter his lover in small increments. He studied Ray's face, looking for any sign of pain, until he was fully seated. Ray was tighter than he'd guessed and Deacon had never felt anything quite so intense in his life.

"Breathe," he told Ray, wishing he could take his own advice.

"I've never been so full," Ray panted.

"Am I hurting you?" *Please don't ask me to pull out*, Deacon silently begged.

Ray shook his head and grinned. "You're killing me, but in a good way."

Relieved that he wasn't the only one feeling the intense pleasure, Deacon moaned. He felt Ray's muscles begin to relax so Deacon began to move. He started a slow rhythm in and out until he made certain he wasn't hurting his lover.

Ray gazed into Deacon's eyes and nodded, giving silent permission for more. Deacon lifted his torso off Ray's and began to thrust faster, surging deep, before pulling out. With every pump of his hips, Deacon felt like he was losing himself to the smaller man.

There had been too much teasing for him to last long, but Deacon intended to make a lasting impression. He reached back and hooked Ray's legs with his arms, opening Ray further.

"Yes!" Ray panted. "I feel you. Oh fuck, I feel you!"

The younger man was gasping for breath as Deacon relentlessly assaulted the sweet body of his lover over and over. He was rewarded with a cry of ecstasy as Ray climaxed.

Deacon knew he was riding the edge, but when Ray's body tightened around his cock, he was lost. He buried his crown as deep into Ray's body as he could and filled the condom, howling Ray's name as he came.

He released Ray's legs and kissed his lover as the aftershocks continued to rack his body. He wanted to whisper sweet nothings in Ray's ear, but what could he say that didn't sound trite? It was the God's honest truth that he'd never experienced anything as good as what had just happened, but he knew words were cheap, especially after fucking.

Deacon reached down and held the base of the condom as he pulled out of Ray. He gave Ray a quick, deep kiss before climbing off the bed and heading for the bathroom.

After disposing of the soiled rubber and cleaning his dick in the sink, he ran a washcloth under the hot tap and carried it back to the bedroom. Ray was sound asleep, his breathing still more labored than normal.

Deacon cleaned his lover as much as he could without waking him and turned off the bedside lamp. He drew the covers over them and settled Ray against his chest. As much as he would've enjoyed soft kisses and a bit of pillow talk, he knew it was better Ray had fallen asleep.

"It's too soon," he mumbled to himself.

Chapter Five

༺༻

Ray spent the majority of the following three days in his father's office, researching on the internet. He glanced at the time on the bottom of the monitor and cursed. If he was going to make his meeting with his dad's lawyer, he needed to get going.

He bookmarked the page he'd been reviewing and pushed away from the desk. From his research so far, he definitely saw the possibilities of his plans coming to fruition, but he'd need some money to make it happen.

Although nostalgic, the summer cabin needed work, along with several of the other cabins. He also felt the hired hands deserved nicer homes. He'd heard grumbles about how cold the houses were in the winter. The way he figured it, it would take a pretty good sum of money to do the job right and still keep the integrity of the older homes. He'd heard about a company in Kansas City that made new windows that looked like the originals. Ray had gone as far as to contact the people. In his opinion, the single-pane windows were the biggest culprits of the drafty cabins.

The guilt he felt over hoping there was some cash involved with his father's estate had slowly been replaced with the knowledge that he could do wonderful things for the J Bar with the money. Not just the ranch itself, but the cowboys who'd come to regard the land as their home. Advertising alone for their new venture was going to be expensive, but Ray knew he had to get ads in a few of the publications catering to the GLBT community.

He grabbed the keys to his rental car off the table and opened the door, surprised when Taggert almost knocked on his face. "Whoa."

Shocked, Taggert lowered his hand. "Sorry. I was just coming to see you. Deacon said you were headed into Red Lodge and I wondered if I could catch a ride."

"Sure, but I don't know how long I'll be." Ray led the way to the sedan.

"I don't mind waiting. I've got an appointment at the clinic."

After they were both buckled in, Ray pulled down the drive. He wondered if he could use the unexpected opportunity to get Taggert's opinion on the changes he was about to propose to the others.

Ray waited until they were on the county road headed toward Red Lodge. "So, um, can I ask your opinion on something?"

Taggert was only around twenty-two and seemed surprised to be asked. "Me? Sure."

"What would you think about opening the ranch for primarily gay and lesbian guests? You know, someplace they could vacation and be themselves."

"We already have that. Not many, mind you, but there are the occasional guests who're gay."

"Yes, but I'm talking more about blocking off months when we're exclusively marketing trips for them. Trips where they're allowed to be themselves without worrying who might catch them kissing or holding a lover's hand."

Taggert rubbed the back of his neck, under the wide brim of his hat. "I think it sounds good, but you're talking about a lot of temptation coming and going from the ranch. You know the policies in place."

Ray chuckled. "I do and I hate them. One of the reasons I'm interested in doing this is so everyone can relax and be who they are, not just the guests."

Taggert seemed to think it over for several minutes before answering. "I've never been *out* out like a lot of the guys. Heck, I've never even been to a bar outside of Red Lodge. Maybe you should ask someone a little more experienced than me."

Ray shook his head. "Experience has nothing to do with it. I guess the real question is would you like to live in an atmosphere of complete acceptance. From the sound of it, you haven't had that up until now."

"Sure. Who wouldn't? But I'm not wearing chaps around the ranch without any jeans on just to give the guests a thrill, so don't even ask," Taggert joked.

Ray laughed and held up a hand. "I promise."

* * * * *

The weekly cattle drive was always a favorite among guests. It wasn't really a big production, just moving head from one pasture to another, but it gave the wannabe cowboys a chance to show what they'd learned during the week.

Despite a kerfuffle with one group of yearlings, it all went rather smoothly. Deacon sat back in the saddle as Neil put on a show for the folks. Deacon had noticed one of the heifers had a sore on her leg that needed to be tended.

With his well-trained Australian Shepherd, Georgia, Neil broke the heifer from the herd and wasted no time roping her. Watching Neil as his gelding ran at top speed was the closest thing to a religious experience most cowboys got, unless, of course, it was the sight of Griggs riding his horse bareback in the buckskins he occasionally put on for the guests.

The tired crowd seemed to appreciate the skill involved and cheered Neil and Georgia on. After one of the older men helped Neil apply ointment to the heifer's injury, Neil did a little showing off for the guests.

Deacon heard the creak of a saddle coming up behind him and glanced over his shoulder.

"Hey," Griggs greeted.

Deacon waited until the horse wrangler brought his horse up beside Black Jack. "Everything going okay?"

Griggs nodded. "I'm a little worried about a couple of the guests taking the ride down the ridge."

"Let me guess, Danny and Judy?"

Griggs searched the small group of riders until his gaze landed on the two people in question. "I don't think they have the confidence to take a plunge like that."

Deacon studied the couple in their twenties. Without taking the horses down the ridge, it was a four-hour ride back to the ranch. "Go talk to them about it. If they honestly don't think they can do it, I'll get 'em home."

"You sure? That'll put you back after dark."

"I'm sure. Just have Mother keep a couple plates warmed for us. As long as we stay on the path, we'll be fine."

Griggs nodded and rode off toward the couple. Deacon watched as Griggs tried to explain what riding down the ridge entailed. Hundreds of inexperienced riders had made the trek just fine, but the key was to trust your horse. The stock on the J Bar was so well trained, they could take the steep downward slope with their eyes closed, but nervous riders had a tendency to pull on the reins, which often spelled trouble.

Griggs looked over at Deacon and shook his head. Deacon could tell the wrangler felt bad, but there was little that could be done about it.

Deacon clicked his tongue and Black Jack rode forward. "We'll go ahead and start back. See you all later."

By the way Judy was sitting the saddle, Deacon had a pretty good idea she would soon be wishing she'd taken the short ride home.

* * * * *

After dropping Taggert by the clinic, Ray parked in front of the Law Office of Krueger and Westmoor. He checked his hair in the rearview mirror before getting out and locking up. He smiled to himself as he hit the key fob again and unlocked the car. He had to keep reminding himself he wasn't in the city.

He stepped into the reception area and smiled at the young woman behind the desk. "Ray Justice. I've an appointment with James Krueger."

"Yes, Mr. Justice, Mr. Krueger is expecting you. Second door on the right down that hall."

"Thank you." Ray walked to the indicated office and knocked on the doorjamb of the open door. "Mr. Krueger?"

A middle-aged man with thinning hair stood and extended his hand. "Nice to meet you. Please call me James."

"Thank you, James." Ray took the offered seat.

James shuffled a few files on his desk, handed Ray a large manila envelope, before opening an additional file folder. "Everything of a personal nature should be in there. I have a few papers for you to sign, including the new deed on the ranch, so I can get it through the court as quickly as possible."

Ray nodded and signed and initialed numerous documents. Most of them had to do with the ranch. He'd yet to see anything about a cash payment, but he assumed that would be in the envelope he'd been given. At the direction his thoughts were headed, Ray had to once again push back the guilt. He knew in his heart the money was needed to enhance the J Bar. He felt confident his dad would be proud of the things he was hoping to accomplish.

After getting the legal paperwork out of the way, Ray stood and shook James' hand. "Thank you for taking the time to track me down. I would've never known about the J Bar if it hadn't been for your phone call."

A strange expression crossed James' face momentarily before being wiped away with a forced smile. "I wish you the best of luck, Ray."

Ray nodded to the receptionist on his way back to his car. As soon as he was safely ensconced in the privacy of the sedan, he opened the large envelope. He was surprised to find a few pictures of himself along with a single, smaller envelope with his name written on the outside in his father's handwriting.

With shaking hands, Ray tore open the white business-sized envelope. He unfolded the piece of notebook paper and began to read.

Ray Jr.,

If you're reading this, I must be dead. It's sad that it took my death and the hope of money to bring you to Montana, but here you are.

As I'm sure you are aware, the ranch has been left to you. I have to be honest and say it wasn't what I would have wanted given a choice. You've never given a fuck about me or your heritage here in Montana, but the legalities are such that I can't bequeath it to anyone but you.

Everything I did have a choice in, I've left to Deacon and a few of the other ranch hands. They deserve what they got and more, so don't you dare try to sue them to get what you feel should be yours, or so help me God, I'll haunt you until the day you die.

Ray gasped at the vehemence behind the words written in his dad's handwriting. He almost tore the letter up right then and there, but some perverse side of him continued reading.

I know legally, I can't stop you from selling the ranch and heading back to your fancy life in New York, but I'm asking you to please take some time to reconsider. The J Bar has been in my family for generations. We've always taken great pride in having one of the largest privately owned ranches in the state of Montana.

If you just go on back east, Deacon and the rest of the crew are more than qualified to run the place. You'll earn a steady income from the profits and you'll never have to dirty your soft hands lifting a finger to earn it.

That was as far as Ray could bring himself to go. He stuffed the letter into the large envelope and threw it into the backseat, out of his sight.

It took him several moments to calm down enough to get the key in the ignition. As he pulled away from the curb toward the coffeehouse where he'd agreed to meet Taggert, he fought off tears.

He kept telling himself over and over it didn't matter. RJ didn't know the story behind why Ray had never written or come out to Montana to see him. Things would've been different if only he hadn't been lied to by the people who were supposed to love him the most.

Taggert stepped out of the cute storefront as soon as Ray pulled up, two cups of steaming coffee in his hands. Ray leaned across the console and opened the passenger door.

"Thanks." Taggert handed Ray his cup. "One sugar and two creams, right?"

Ray nodded and settled the botanic-printed cup in the console. As he drove out of town, he had no doubt Taggert was able to pick up on his current mood, because the cowboy didn't even attempt conversation.

The sun was quickly setting and Ray adjusted his visor, cursing himself for leaving his sunglasses on the dresser. As he drove, he reached down and lifted his cup, hoping it had cooled off enough to drink.

"Watch out!" Taggert yelled as Ray rounded a corner.

As if in slow motion, the cup of hot coffee dropped out of his hand as he tried too late to swerve around the large bull elk.

Ray felt the impact moments before his world went black.

* * * * *

They were only about a quarter mile from the ranch when Deacon was surprised to see Neil riding at top speed toward them. Even from a distance, Deacon could tell by Neil's body language that something was wrong.

He gave Black Jack a nudge and took off toward the cowboss. "What's happened?" he yelled when he got close enough. Both men pulled their horses to a stop.

"We just got a call from Beartooth Hospital. There was an accident on the way home from Red Lodge. Taggert and Ray are both being brought in."

Deacon didn't even wait for further details, he ran Black Jack toward the barn at an all-out gallop. Jimmy and Griggs were both waiting by the barn when Deacon rode up. Jimmy had thought ahead and had Deacon's truck running and waiting.

Deacon hopped into the truck and floored it, spraying dirt everywhere in his haste to get to the hospital. Halfnway down the driveway, Deacon was forced to slow the truck and put on his seat belt.

Once he was on the county road, he drove as fast as he dared toward Red Lodge. About halfway to town, he spotted flashing lights. He slowed to a crawl as the traffic all but stopped to gawk at the accident scene. It was a sick thing to do, but Deacon knew it was human nature.

A tow truck was loading what was left of Ray's rental car onto a flatbed, the entire front of the sedan crumpled. Deacon's first thought was Ray had hit a tree, but the blood and gore just past the wrecker proved him wrong. "Fuck."

Clear of the accident, Deacon passed as many cars as he could safely in an effort to get to Ray. "Please, God, let them be okay."

* * * * *

Even before he opened his eyes, he felt the weight of someone's hand on his upper arm. He knew it was Deacon by the smell of horses and leather. "Hey," he rasped, opening his eyes.

"Hey, babe. How're you feeling?"

Ray licked his lips. "Thirsty."

Deacon reached for a plastic cup on the small table and directed a straw to Ray's mouth. "Just a couple of sips. We don't want you upchucking all over the place."

As much as he wanted to drink the entire glass, Ray followed Deacon's orders. "What happened? What the hell was that thing?"

"Bull elk," Deacon informed Ray. "When you decide to hit an animal, you sure as hell know how to go for the biggest ones we got."

"Shouldn't that be in a zoo or something instead of wandering around the road willy-nilly?"

Deacon grinned. "Hey, you're talking about the pride of Montana right there."

Ray looked down at himself, surprised to see he appeared to have all his parts intact. "How bad am I?"

"Concussion, broken nose, sprained wrist and a hell of a burn on your thigh."

"Coffee."

"Huh? You want coffee?"

"No, I was trying to drink coffee. I must've spilled it. How's Taggert?"

Deacon squirmed in his seat. "Broken arm and collarbone, bruises, a few minor cuts. There's one on his eyebrow that he was worried about, but I assured him it would make him even sexier."

Ray narrowed his eyes. "Don't you go getting ideas about Taggert."

Deacon chuckled. He leaned in and placed a soft kiss on Ray's lips. "No need to worry. Someone else has my full attention at the moment."

It wasn't until some of the fog left Ray's brain that he remembered why he'd gone into Red Lodge in the first place. With no money to start the new venture, he knew the last few days had been wasted. "Will I be well enough to go home in the morning?"

"What? I thought you weren't leaving until Sunday."

Ray didn't know how to tell Deacon the truth. He needed time away from Montana, the J Bar and Deacon to process all that had happened. "I have a few things I need to do before I have to work on Monday."

Deacon blinked several times. "It's that important that you get back to the city?"

Ray tried to nod but winced as his head felt like it was ready to fall off his neck. "Please, just promise me you'll get me to the airport in the morning."

The muscles in Deacon's jaws started pulsing as he ground his teeth. "Sure, but you know, hitting elk isn't an everyday occurrence around here. You don't really need to run back to New York because of it."

Ray reached out and threaded his fingers through Deacon's. "I have some thinking I need to do, please."

What would Deacon say if he knew Ray needed to decide if refurbishing his father's ranch was worth selling the house his mom had worked so hard to pay off? No. That wasn't exactly true. He knew deep down he needed time to digest the letter his dad had written.

He knew RJ had been hurt by Ray's apparent lack of understanding, but had he really tried to reach out? The more he thought about it, the madder he became. Not once had his dad tried to see him face-to-face.

"Hey, what's going on inside that bruised head of yours?" Deacon whispered, kissing Ray's cheek.

"Just wondering why my dad never tried to see me. When I found out the truth, I was so angry with my mom for lying to him. But I think if I were a dad, I would've done everything in my power to see my son, whether he approved of me or not. I would've at least tracked him down once he became an adult and had a man-to-man conversation with him."

Deacon's eyes were filled with sorrow as he smoothed the once spiked hair away from Ray's forehead. "He had more pride than any man I've ever known, sometimes to a fault. He was my best friend, but even I've had a few choice words for him lately. What he did was wrong, point blank, and I won't make excuses for him."

Deacon leaned farther in and nuzzled Ray's neck. "You mean the world to me. If you have to go back to New York, don't stay away long. I've kinda gotten used to you."

Ray appreciated everything his lover said, but if his feelings for Deacon were real, they would survive the time it took for him to get his head and heart straightened out. Ray reached out and cupped Deacon's cheek. Here was a man he'd known less than a week, yet Deacon meant more to him than anyone else in the world.

As much as he wanted to tell the man he loved those three little words, his conscience wouldn't let him. Maybe it was time to figure out who *he* was, not what his mother, or father, thought he was.

Chapter Six

Ray's boss came into his office and tossed a folder onto his desk. "Cows? I ask you for an ad campaign for a bakery and you give me cows!"

Ray glanced up from his computer. "It's head."

"Excuse me?"

"Head or cattle, not cows. The whole premise of the ad is taking people back to the country. To a time when mothers baked for their families."

The red-faced man in front of him growled. "You haven't given me anything but cattle and cowboys since you've been back from your vacation."

"It wasn't a vacation. My father died."

"Whatever. Why don't you take a few days off and decide where it is you want to be. This isn't the country. You can't do local advertising geared toward the people of Manhattan with these silly ads you keep coming up with."

Ray watched as his boss stormed out of his office. "Fuck."

He leaned back in his chair and closed his eyes. He knew his boss was right. At that moment he longed to be on the front porch of his house on the J Bar. The heat in the city was stifling. What he wouldn't give for a shady spot in the country with a cool breeze.

Although he'd been back for nearly two weeks, he'd decided almost immediately he wanted to go back. But things took time. He had a house to sell and a life to rearrange.

* * * * *

"Hey, boss?"

Deacon glanced up from the schedule book in front of him. "Yeah, Jimmy?"

"This came for Ray. The rental car place in Billings finally came to haul away what was left of Ray's rental. These are his personal effects that were found inside."

Deacon took the large manila envelope and set it beside him. "Thanks."

Jimmy nodded and left the cookhouse.

"You want me to make another pot of coffee?" Martha asked.

Deacon tipped his cup, surprised to see his coffee had gone cold. "That'd be great."

He still had at least another hour of work to do and knew he'd need the caffeine to keep him awake. How he'd managed to get so attached to Ray, he still didn't understand, but life without his lover was taking its toll on his sleeping habits.

His finger brushed the corner of the envelope. The address at the top left corner told him it was from RJ's lawyer. "It's not any of your business, Deacon."

"You say something?" Martha asked, coming into the room.

"No. Just talking to myself."

Martha set a fresh carafe of coffee in front of him. Instead of moving off, she took a seat across the dining room table. "He got under your skin, didn't he?"

Deacon grinned. "Is it that obvious?"

"Well, I could tell you no and save your pride, or I could tell the truth. Which would you prefer?"

"I miss him. Talking on the phone isn't the same."

"So tell him."

Deacon looked at the woman who'd mothered all of them at one time or another. "I can't. I don't think it's me he's staying away from. I think it's whatever's in this envelope."

Martha eyed the envelope in question. "Guess you have a decision to make."

Deacon nodded and poured himself more coffee. "Even though Ray was RJ's son, I think my old friend hated him." Deacon went on to tell Martha about the letters Ray had found, as well as the letter Deacon had received.

"...I just don't understand him," Deacon concluded.

Martha reached across the table and covered Deacon's hand. "I think in the end, when RJ knew he was dying, he became bitter about all the things that had gone wrong in his life, namely Ray. It was the hurt he felt in those letters. Don't let them cloud your judgment when it comes to his friendship. He truly was your friend. You're letting his relationship with Ray taint those memories."

"Do you think he really loved Ray, ever?"

Martha shrugged. "He took that answer to his grave." She stood and tapped her fingers on the table. "Maybe it's up to you to make this place Ray's home and not RJ's."

"What do you mean?" Deacon knew he'd made Ray feel welcomed at the ranch.

"RJ put his stamp on everything around here. Ghosts have a way of keeping away the living. If there are bad feelings between RJ and Ray, maybe it's time things changed."

"Like?" he prodded.

Martha braced her hands on the table and leaned toward Deacon. "In the old days, ranches were named after the brand they carried. J Bar was the brand for this place, but we don't brand the cattle anymore, we tag them."

"And?"

"I happen to know Elijah Justice stated in his will the J Bar could never be passed to anyone other than a Justice. He said nothing about the land, just the name. I think it's pretty clear Ray will probably never have an heir. What's going to happen to this place when it's his time to go? Maybe a visit to Mr.

Krueger would help you find some answers to your problem with Ray. Make this place Ray's home and he'll come back."

Deacon scratched his jaw. He knew from reading RJ's letters the last thing he wanted was to pass the ranch to Ray, so why was this topic coming up now? "Why didn't you tell RJ about your theories on the J Bar?"

Martha smiled. "Because unlike the rest of you, I knew about Ray and I didn't want RJ to leave the ranch to anyone but the last Justice. It's the way it should be, regardless of their relationship. You seem to forget how long I've worked here. There aren't many Justice skeletons that I don't know about."

Without a self-satisfied smile, Martha turned and walked back into the kitchen to finish preparing lunch.

Deacon picked up the envelope and emptied its contents onto the table. If he was going to see Mr. Krueger, he needed to understand what he was up against.

* * * * *

Ray finished taping the box and piled it onto the stack with the others. He'd made good headway over the last several days. He'd made arrangements with one of the local charities for a pick-up the following day and he only had half the attic left to sort.

He hadn't had much luck selling his mother's house, but the market sucked and he knew that when he'd put it up for sale. With the forced time off from his job, he'd decided to do what he could to ready the old place.

The chiming of the doorbell drew his attention away from the task at hand. He stood and brushed the accumulated dust from his shirt and hair before climbing down the ladder.

Before he could make his way downstairs, someone began pounding.

"I'm coming," he yelled.

He opened the door and nearly fainted. The man he couldn't get out of his head stood not a foot in front of him. Ray launched himself into his lover's arms and kissed him.

When he started to pull away enough to question Deacon, his man's arms tightened and took the kiss deeper. Ray opened his mouth and sucked his lover's tongue inside. Damn, he'd missed Deacon's taste. The kiss went even hotter as Deacon lapped at Ray's lips, chin and cheeks with his tongue. Within moments, Ray's cock was hard and grinding against Deacon's thigh as they continued their erotic tongue-play.

Ray pulled Deacon into the house and shut the door. "Need you," he broke away from the kiss long enough to say.

Deacon bent and put his shoulder to Ray's midsection, lifting him off the ground. In his current position, Ray had a perfect view of Deacon's ass, encased in a faded pair of jeans. He ran his hands over the cowboy's firm buns as he was carried up the stairs. He couldn't get his hand inside Deacon's waistband, but he could run his fingers up the seam between the cheeks of his lover's ass. "Which one?" Deacon asked.

"First door," Ray replied.

Deacon tossed Ray onto the bed. "Stuff?"

Ray bit his bottom lip. "Condoms are in the bathroom, still in my shaving kit." He slid out the bedside drawer. "I've got lube though."

While Deacon went to retrieve the condoms, Ray began stripping out of his clothes. By the time a nude Deacon walked back into the room, sheathed and ready, Ray had already started stretching himself. He hadn't taken the time to get the dildo out of the drawer, instead doing things the old-fashioned way. It seemed both of them were in a hurry.

Ray grinned, inserting another finger as Deacon climbed onto the bed. "What're you doing here?"

Deacon stopped and grinned, gesturing toward the door. "Should I leave?"

Reining in the Past

"Hell no." He removed his fingers and spread his legs. "Come closer."

Deacon insinuated himself between Ray's thighs and guided the head of his cock to Ray's hole. "You remember our agreement?"

Ray knew exactly what Deacon was asking. "I promise to tell you if it hurts."

After pushing the head through the ring of muscles, Deacon stopped and leaned down for a kiss. Of all the erotic kisses they'd shared in their relationship, Ray knew there was something incredibly different about this one. He knew he wasn't the only one who felt it. The low moan coming from Deacon as their tongues twined was also different.

Ray opened his eyes and stared up at the handsome man he'd missed beyond reason. No words were spoken, but Ray felt the connection between them deepen even further.

Without breaking eye contact, Deacon began to move. In a slow rocking motion, Deacon worked his length inside Ray's body. Although he felt a few twinges, Ray concentrated to keep his face from showing it. Having Deacon with him was too important to let anything ruin the moment.

Once buried to the root, Deacon leaned down and swiped his tongue across Ray's lips. "God, I've missed this, you. My entire adult life's been spent on the ranch and never have I felt lonelier than the last two weeks."

Ray nodded. He knew what Deacon was talking about. The time spent away from Deacon had been pure hell. It hadn't mattered that he'd kept himself busy. There hadn't been a minute of the day he wasn't tempted to say "fuck it all" and go back to Montana.

Deacon withdrew his cock and slid back in. The stretch was amazing. Ray would swear he felt each protruding vein of Deacon's thick cock.

Ray wrapped his legs higher around his lover's torso as he moaned with each thrust. The words that he'd been dying to say sat on the tip of his tongue. *Not yet.*

Deacon changed position as the intensity level increased. Although Ray missed the scratch of Deacon's pubic hair against his cock, he enjoyed being able to look up at his cowboy's gorgeous face.

He grinned as Deacon's dark eyebrows knitted together, as if concentrating with everything he had. Ray knew he was the recipient of all that concentration and it served to excite him even more.

The sound of skin slapping skin as Deacon's heavy sac swung against Ray's ass was almost deafening in the room. Who would have thought he could even miss that sound? Was there anything about the man fucking his brains out that he hadn't longed for over the past couple of weeks?

Deacon grabbed Ray by the ankles and spread his legs farther apart as he continued to pound in and out of Ray's willing hole. Deacon gazed into Ray's eyes. "Damn, I've missed you."

Ray knew he had completely fallen head over heels for the man as he stared at the almost tangible emotions visible in Deacon's expression. While one hand was busy on his cock, Ray lifted the other to wipe some of the sweat from Deacon's face. Once again, Ray wanted to tell Deacon how much he loved him, but he knew it would mean more when the two of them weren't fucking like bunnies.

His hand traveled to Deacon's chest as he scraped the lightly furred skin with his short fingernails. The sight of the red marks visible under the hair sent a thrill racing through Ray's body. It was yet another reminder that Deacon was really there. His lover had actually traveled to New York to be with him.

"Deacon," he gasped as his cock erupted, shooting strings of seed onto his stomach.

Deacon's gaze was riveted downward. Ray wasn't sure if it was the sight of him coming or the red scratches marking Deacon's chest, but something seemed to set his lover off.

Deacon roared with a combination of growl and grunt as he hammered his cock in and out of Ray.

With his wits once again intact, Ray studied Deacon's face as he buried himself to the root and jerked with each spurt of cum. Ray took control and lowered his legs, once again wrapping them around Deacon's waist as he pulled his cowboy down on top of him.

It didn't matter that Deacon weighed at least fifty pounds more than Ray did, the press of his lover's body against him was more than welcome, it was needed. Ray ran his hands across Deacon's back as his partner struggled to catch his breath.

Ray knew he couldn't hold back any longer. He positioned his lips at Deacon's ear and whispered, "I love you."

Deacon turned his head and captured Ray's mouth in a deep kiss. After delving deep, Deacon peppered Ray's lips and face with kisses. "I love you, too."

Ray almost whimpered when Deacon's flaccid cock left his hole. Deacon rolled over and removed the condom, disposing of it in the waste bin beside the bed.

Their cleanup forgotten for the moment, Ray curled himself against Deacon's chest. "So are you going to tell me why you came all the way to New York?"

Deacon ran his fingertips down the side of Ray's face. "I have some paperwork for you to sign and a business proposition."

Confused, Ray leaned up on his elbow to stare down at Deacon. "I thought I'd already signed everything."

Deacon shook his head. "I've been working with Mr. Krueger. He drew up the papers to have the ranch renamed. It won't be official until it goes through the courts and stuff, but we can't do anything without your approval and signature."

"What're you talking about? Why would you want to rename the J Bar?"

Deacon pulled Ray back down into his arms. "It's a legal way to get around your great-great-grandfather's stubbornness. The ranch is yours now. Not your dad's. Not your ancestors'. Yours."

"So what name did you decide on?" Even after such a short amount of time, Ray couldn't imagine the ranch being called anything other than the J Bar.

Deacon's expression brightened. "Well, it's still up to you, of course, but the other hands and I thought Justice River had a nice ring to it."

"Justice River." Ray rolled the name around on his tongue. "I like it."

"So you'll come back home with me?"

"All the changes I have in mind for the ranch will cost money. I can't do any of them until I can get my mom's house sold."

"Hang on a sec." Deacon climbed out of bed and disappeared into the bathroom. He came back out with a damp towel draped over one broad shoulder and his wallet.

"Thanks, but there's really no need to pay me for sex. I'll give it to you free," Ray joked.

Deacon tossed the towel at Ray before sitting on the bed beside him. He pulled a check out of the wallet and handed it to Ray. "Your employees have a proposition for you."

Ray stared at the check, dumfounded. "What's this for?"

"Well, we thought maybe you'd let us buy in to the dude ranch side of the business," Deacon informed him.

"But what if it flops? This has to be everyone's savings. I can't risk everyone's money," Ray tried to explain.

"Why? You're willing to risk your own. What's the difference? We'll all have a vested interest in making the business profitable." Deacon shrugged. "Besides, we believe in you. And this way, the cowboys will feel a sense of permanence they haven't felt before."

"What about you?" Ray asked.

"What *about* me?"

"Will this give you a reason to stick around for the long haul?" Ray bit his bottom lip, waiting.

"No," Deacon said with a shake of his head.

Ray's chest tightened.

Deacon leaned in for a kiss. "But this will."

"Good answer." Ray kissed Deacon and pushed him back onto the mattress for round two.

* * * * *

Ray was directing the movers when a large box van pulled into his drive. The side of the van said Reconstruction Specialists with the slogan *We Fix it Right the Second Time Around*.

An older man climbed out and walked toward Ray. "Ray Justice?"

Ray nodded. "That's me. You must be Walter."

"Yep. Have the windows been delivered yet?"

"They came a few hours ago. I told the deliverymen to put them in the hay barn. I hope that's okay."

"That's great. My son and I can sort through and determine which ones go to which cabin."

With the angle of the sun bouncing off the van's windshield, Ray hadn't noticed anyone else in the van. Now that he looked again, sure enough a younger man sat in the passenger seat.

"We're putting you up in the cabin next to the cookhouse. It's only one big room and a bathroom, but there are two beds, a fireplace and a couple of comfortable leather chairs. The cookhouse is always open if you're in need of something to drink or a midnight snack. Just make sure and clean up your mess or Martha will tan your hide."

Walter nodded. "I'm a bit of a neat freak myself, so Martha and I should get along just fine."

Ray chuckled. "Don't say that too loud. Martha's been trying to hunt up a man for the last thirty years."

Walter laughed, but Ray detected a twinkle in the man's blue eyes. Looking up at the sky, Walter shielded his eyes. "Which cabin would you like me and Tyson to start on?"

"Well, it kind of depends on how long it's going to take for each one. The summer cabin has the most windows, but it won't be empty for another four days. After that, you'll only have a week until more guests are due to arrive."

Walter pulled a faded blue bandana out of his back pocket and wiped his brow. "We'll go around and take a look at everything. I should be able to have a schedule to you by evening."

"Sounds good."

Walter shook Ray's hand once more before returning to his vehicle. Ray strolled back to the house, sidestepping one of the movers carrying an end table. He was glad he'd let Deacon talk him into shuffling some of RJ's furniture to the other cabins.

As he walked into the house, he smiled. The place did feel a lot more like home with some of his stuff scattered around. The big leather-and-tapestry couch he'd saved three months for fit perfectly in front of the fireplace. He couldn't wait for winter nights spent snuggled up with Deacon in front of a roaring fire.

"Wow, I barely recognize the place."

Ray glanced over his shoulder as strong arms wrapped around his waist. "Who knew my taste ran to rustic log cabin? I thought I was being all Pottery Barn-ish."

"Pottery Barn-ish?" Deacon questioned.

"It's a yuppy store. Forget it." Ray leaned back against Deacon's chest. "The window guys got in."

"Yeah, I'm the one who directed them down here." Deacon kissed Ray's neck. "That son of Walter's is quite the looker."

Ray turned and narrowed his eyes. "Haven't we already had this conversation?"

Deacon gave Ray a quick kiss. "I have a strong feeling we're going to have good-looking men all over the place in a couple of months. Let's agree to look, appreciate, but never touch."

Ray pretended to think about it for a few moments. "No touching?"

"Promise. No touching."

"Okay. So tell me what Tyson looks like and don't leave out any good parts."

Epilogue

It had been a long, hard winter and Ray wasn't sure his balls would ever truly thaw out. He put on his straw cowboy hat and sunglasses and left the house. He was still amazed at the personal changes he'd undergone in the previous seven months. Not only had Deacon moved in with him before winter set in, but Ray had forgiven his father and learned to ride a horse without getting saddle sore.

"You'd better get that skinny ass in gear if you want to greet our first guests," Deacon hollered down the ranch road.

Ray rolled his eyes and continued at his normal stride. "Cool cowboys don't run," he yelled back.

He was happy to see Tyson standing on the cookhouse porch. Everyone had been so impressed by the job he'd done on the windows and the way he got along with the cowboys, they'd hired him to perform routine maintenance on the ranch.

As he passed the porch, Ray beckoned to the good-looking man. "Come on, we're greeting the guests as a family."

Tyson grinned and took the steps two at a time, joining Ray in no time. "I wasn't sure."

Ray wrapped his arm around Tyson's waist. "Well, now you are. You're as much a part of this as any of us."

He started to drop his arm, but Tyson nudged him in the ribs. "Keep it there. I love to hear Deacon growl."

"You're evil, but I love it."

Sure enough, by the time they made it to the barn, Deacon's eyes were narrowed. "You stepping in on me, Tyson?"

Tyson chuckled, the sound vibrating Ray's chest. "No. Just testing to make sure you still know what you've got."

Deacon pulled Ray away from Tyson. "I know. Don't you worry your pretty little head about it."

The comment, combined with Tyson's incredible size, had the other hands laughing when the dark blue passenger van came into view.

"Look alive, boys." Deacon wrapped an arm around Ray. "You did it, babe. Our first group where we can all feel completely comfortable with who we are."

Ray leaned against his lover. Their schedule still wasn't completely booked, but it was early days.

The van pulled up and parked. Griggs climbed out, red faced. Instead of waiting for the guests to get out of the van, he walked straight over to Ray and Deacon. "You need to keep that kid away from me or his first day on the ranch is gonna be his last."

Ray looked around Griggs and spotted a man in his early twenties stealing glances at Griggs. The guest's shoulder-length, shiny black curls bounced around his face as he helped unload the luggage. "He's cute."

"He's a pain in my ass. All the way here he was asking one question after another. He fancies himself quite the horseman. It's been my experience that those who talk about it don't know shit. And that guy won't shut up."

Ray grinned and reached out to thump Griggs on the shoulder. "You've got your first guest crush. How cute."

Griggs made a disgusted sound and walked off.

Ray glanced from the cute man ogling Griggs up to Deacon. "Griggs is so screwed."

"Yep." Deacon bent down and gave Ray a quick kiss. "Let's go welcome the future of Justice River Ranch."

BAREBACK COWBOY

Chapter One

☙

Ethan Griggs grumbled under his breath as he waited for the last flight to arrive. The other eight guests were already loaded into the back of the van along with their luggage, but one of the planes had been delayed and the men were getting restless.

He checked his watch and pushed away from the side of the van he'd been leaning on. He stuck his head through the open window and addressed his passengers. "I'll be back."

Because of the flight delay, Griggs had been forced to park the van in the lot instead of out front where he normally picked up guests. As he made his way to the terminal building, he grabbed the pack of cigarettes from his front pocket and lit up. He wasn't supposed to smoke around the guests, but he was in dire need.

He stopped outside the door and stood in the small smoking section as he inhaled. The rush of menthol and nicotine into his bloodstream seemed to calm him immediately.

The sidewalk was busy with people going in and out of the terminal, but Griggs zeroed in on a sweet-looking young stud in low-rise jeans and a cowboy hat. The guy was patting his pockets, one after the other. He was obviously looking for his lighter.

Griggs walked over and held a flame in front of the cowboy. "Need a light?"

The young guy looked up at Griggs, flashing a set of deep dimples. "Thanks."

Griggs was struck by the intense gray eyes that stared back at him. Rimmed by long, thick, black lashes, the kid was to die for. Too bad he was so damn young.

The cowboy stuck out his hand. "I'm Bridger."

Griggs started to shake the man's hand but stopped. "Bridger Collins?

"Yeah?" Bridger finally dropped his hand.

"I'm Griggs, from Justice River Ranch. I've been waiting for you."

"Really? Cool. The airline got me on a different flight. When I came out and no one was here, I called the ranch to make sure you hadn't left without me."

Griggs winced. He hated cell phones, but Deacon always made him carry one in the van. "Sorry, I've got my phone turned off."

Bridger shrugged and took another drag of his cigarette.

Griggs noticed the duffle at Bridger's sneakered feet. "Did the rest of your luggage not make it?"

Bridger exhaled and picked up his bag. "This is it. Boots, couple pairs of jeans, shirts, socks, underwear and my meds."

Meds? "Are you sick?"

"No. I've got diabetes, but I've lived with it most of my life."

Griggs stuffed his cigarette into the nearest receptacle and gestured toward the parking lot. "Van's over there."

Bridger put his cigarette out as well and followed Griggs. "So how far is it to the ranch?"

"About an hour. We'll stop at a little place on the way for lunch."

"How many guests will you have this week?"

Griggs glanced at the hot younger cowboy.

"I've got nine including you. Another one of the ranch employees picked up a load of guests from one of the hotels here in Billings."

They reached the van to cheers of excitement. *Yeah, the guests had obviously been about to revolt.* Griggs took Bridger's bag and stuffed it into the back with the rest of the luggage. He still couldn't get over how little Bridger had packed. Most guests barely managed to make the airline's weight limit with their luggage.

He closed the split rear doors and climbed into the driver's seat. "Buckle up," he informed his passengers as he pulled out of the parking lot.

Beside him, Bridger turned around to address the rest of the van. "I'm Bridger Collins. Thank y'all for waiting for me."

One by one, the men introduced themselves. Griggs knew by the end of the week new bonds would be formed by the virtual strangers. He'd heard of friendships lasting for years. People may joke about city folks playing cowboys on a Montana dude ranch, but by the second day their butts would realize there's nothing playing about it.

Although the accommodations at Justice River were top notch, it was still a working cattle ranch. Guests paid a pretty penny to experience the life of a rancher and that's exactly what they received.

Griggs concentrated on the road as he drove out of Billings toward Red Lodge.

"What stock breed does the ranch run?" Bridger asked.

"Angus." Griggs glanced sideways at the gorgeous younger man. "Have you been around cattle?"

"Yeah." Bridger swung his feet up to rest on the dashboard. "My dad has some."

Griggs tightened his grip on the steering wheel as Bridger too off his hat, releasing silky black curls. The kid shook his head before turning to grin at Griggs, flashing those sexy dimples again.

"Damn, that feels better. Mom made me promise to keep it out of sight until I got here. Guess she thought I might have some trouble along the way." Bridger dropped the well-worn straw hat to the floor between their seats.

Griggs returned his attention to the road. He knew exactly what kind of trouble the kid was likely to get himself into and definitely didn't have time to go looking for trouble.

* * * * *

"Is this Roscoe?" Bridger asked.

"That's what the sign said," Griggs grumbled.

Bridger rolled his eyes at the cantankerous cowboy. Since leaving Billings he'd done his best to engage the stud in conversation, but he'd only managed to get one- and two-word replies.

"Cute," Bridger commented as the van parked in front of a stone and log restaurant.

"They've got good food." Griggs opened the door and climbed out.

Before sliding out of the passenger seat, Bridger adjusted his half-hard cock. Grouchy or not, the tall Native American was doing a number on his libido.

He followed a few of the men inside. It wasn't surprising to him that he appeared to be the youngest of the group. He didn't mind. Except for attending classes, he rarely spent time round people his own age.

The small group of guests gathered in front of the hostess stand as Griggs talked to a woman he appeared to know rather well. A laugh erupted from the gorgeous cowboy, surprising Bridger. He wondered how often Griggs actually let his control slip enough to cut up and have fun.

They were shown to a long table at the back of the restaurant. Bridger took a chair, noticing the way Griggs stood back until everyone was seated. There were two empty spots, one next to him and one at the opposite end of the table. He met the black eyes of the cowboy and waited.

After a slight raise of his eyebrows, Griggs sat as far away from Bridger as he could get. The subtle dismissal stung, but Bridger wasn't about to let Griggs know. He turned to the man on his left. "Pete, right?"

The thin, older man nodded. "Pete Allenbrand."

"So where're you from?" Bridger asked, his gaze flicking toward Griggs.

"D.C.," Griggs answered.

"Wow. That's cool. You work for the government or something?"

"No. I'm a school teacher. I've been saving for a trip like this for years. I always had dreams of being a cowboy, but being raised in the city…" Pete shrugged. "Anyway, I decided to fulfill a dream before I got too old to enjoy myself."

Bridger passed a menu to Pete. "I can understand the dream of being a cowboy. It's what I've always wanted, but my father has other plans for me."

"You in school?"

Bridger almost laughed when Pete looked over the top of his glasses at him. Yep. The guy was definitely a teacher. "Yeah. Right now I'm at A&M, but I hate every minute of it."

"Not the right school?"

"Not the right environment." His napkin fell off his lap. When he bent over to retrieve the red and white checked cloth, spots danced across his vision. Bridger decided on the hot beef sandwich and gave the waitress his order.

"Excuse me," Bridger said. With all the excitement, he'd forgotten his insulin bag in the van. He stopped beside Griggs. "Is the van unlocked?"

Griggs nodded. "Something wrong?"

"No. I just forgot something." He'd never been embarrassed of his disease, but announcing it to a table full of strangers didn't make him comfortable either. He left the restaurant and opened the back of the van.

Luckily his duffle was on top of the pile so it didn't take him long to find the black leather bag inside. Insulin kit in hand, he walked back into the restaurant. "Excuse me, ma'am, can you tell me where the restroom is?"

"Sure, sweetie. Just go down that hall, second door on your right."

"Thanks." He entered the restroom and set the kit on the side of the sink as he began washing his hands. He should have known better than to go so long without eating. His levels weren't bad, he already knew that, but he was off his schedule by almost two hours, which wasn't healthy.

Bridger opened the kit and removed his glucose meter and lance. After a quick prick of his finger, he massaged a drop of blood onto the test strip.

As Bridger was digging in the bag for his insulin pen, the door opened. He put his back to the intruder and dialed up the needed dose.

"You okay?" a deep voice asked.

"Yeah." Bridger stood with the pen in his hand. His afternoon injection was always given in his right thigh and he doubted Griggs would appreciate the show. He held up the pen. "I'm overdue for my shot."

"Oh. I'll, uh, leave you to it."

Griggs disappeared and Bridger entered one of the two stalls. He pulled his jeans down and sat on the toilet as he administered the quick prick.

By the time he arrived back to the table, his food had already been delivered. He placed the leather bag under his chair and dug in, aware of Griggs' stare. Bridger wasn't sure if his uneasy feeling had more to do with his glucose level or the penetrating eyes that seemed to study him.

He did his best to concentrate on his lunch, finishing most of the sandwich and a few of the fries. Stares were pretty common in people who hadn't been around someone with type one diabetes. Bridger had gotten used to it, so he rolled with it, determined not to let Griggs' apparent concern go to his head.

The waitress delivered the bills and one by one the group got to their feet to line up at the cash register. In his excitement to get to the ranch, he forgot to grab his kit.

It wasn't until he was in the van and Griggs held it out, that he remembered. "Oh shit. Thanks. I'd have been screwed come suppertime."

Griggs stared at Bridger for several moments, before clearing his throat to address the group. "Justice River Ranch is only two miles or so down the road."

The excitement in the van ratcheted up a notch as the men began to laugh and talk about how full they were.

"Will we get a chance to ride today?" Bridger asked.

Griggs drove under the ranch sign. "Some. Usually your first afternoon is spent getting settled in your rooms. There'll be a meeting in the cookhouse before supper. Then you'll all come out to the barn where I'll help match you up to a horse depending on your skill level."

"I've been riding since I was a kid, so that shouldn't be a problem."

Griggs snorted. "This ain't the fairgrounds, kid. We travel over some pretty rough terrain."

The kid comment stung, but Bridger tried not to let it dampen his enthusiasm. He could tell Griggs was the type of man who didn't take anyone on their word. That was fine with Bridger—he knew his own skills and didn't need to prove them to anyone. Well, except his father, but that issue was better left in Texas.

Bridger braced his hands on the roof of the van to keep from being tossed around like a ragdoll. The dirt and sparsely graveled ranch road was deeply rutted in places and Griggs drove faster than warranted. "Dang, you guys get a lot of run-off up here or what?"

"It's a ranch, not a suburb."

Hot or not, Griggs had a major attitude problem. Maybe the studly cowboy deserved to be taken down a notch or two.

*****

Griggs pulled the van to a stop in front of the barn and jumped out. He walked over to his boss, Deacon. "You need to keep that kid away from me or his first day on the ranch is gonna be his last."

Deacon, the ranch manager and his lover, Ray, the ranch owner, looked around. Ray grinned, evidently spotting Bridger. "He's cute."

"He's a pain in my ass. All the way here he was asking one question after another. He fancies himself quite the horseman. It's been my experience that those who talk about it don't know shit. And that guy won't shut up."

Ray grinned and reached out to thump Griggs on the shoulder. "You've got your first guest crush. How cute."

Griggs made a disgusted sound and walked back toward the van. As long as he kept Bridger at arm's length, he knew he'd be fine. There was something about the young man that just rubbed him the wrong way.

"Wait, wait, wait," Griggs hollered. "We'll unload the luggage in front of your cabins."

The guests nodded and started to put their bags back into the van. Griggs rolled his eyes. He was well off his game. He knew he should have told the guests that very thing before he hastily exited the van.

"Just leave 'em, I'll take care of getting them back in," he told the group. "Why don't you go over and introduce yourselves to the staff?"

After the others had wandered off, Griggs began tossing the suitcases back inside. He heard the other van rumbling down the road as he shut the doors. Although the rest of the staff had witnessed his fuck up, at least Cody hadn't.

As the man in charge of guests, Cody would have given Griggs all kind of shit for his mistake. It wasn't that big of a deal, but Cody loved teasing people. Like a dog with a bone, he was relentless when it came to calling people out for screwing up.

Cody and the rest of the guests hopped out of the van and Griggs moved out of the way. If Griggs was lucky, the entire incident with the baggage wouldn't come up.

"Any trouble?" Cody asked.

Griggs shook his head. "Had one late arrival but nothing serious."

Cody nodded and continued to lead the guests over to Ray and Deacon.

Griggs leaned against the side of the van and waited, using the time to pull the leather thong out of his hair. In a well-practiced move, he smoothed the individual strands with his fingers before pulling it back once again. Once the thong was secured at the nape of his neck, he crossed his arms over his chest.

His gaze continually slid to the young, raven-haired beauty in skin-tight jeans. Griggs chuckled to himself at the expensive sneakers on the kid's feet. If Bridger continued to wear them, they'd be ready for the trash can before the end of the week.

Griggs groaned at the thought of spending an entire week trying to avoid the tempting little morsel. He caught a rather handsome man step up to Bridger and start a conversation. He was too far away to hear what they were talking about but Bridger smiled up at the guy and Griggs felt his stomach tighten.

Dammit! He pushed away from the van and walked across the road to the cookhouse. "Hey, Libby, you got some fresh coffee?"

Libby, the ranch's weekend cook, popped her head out of the kitchen. "Should be safe to drink. Made it about an hour ago."

Griggs grabbed his thermal cup from the top shelf and filled it to the brim. He screwed the cap back on and went to stand at the screen door. After taking a tentative sip, his gaze went back to Bridger.

Griggs unwanted attraction to Bridger probably stemmed from the kid's illness—at least that's what he kept telling himself. Griggs had grown up around diabetes, having a baby sister who had the disease.

How many times had he seen Rachel mess up and forget to check her levels until it was almost too late? Griggs shook his head. From the way Bridger had so carelessly left his leather bag behind at the restaurant, Griggs imagined the kid was no different.

The guests began to break away and filter toward the vans. With another sip of his coffee, Griggs pushed the screen door open and resumed his assigned duties. It felt odd seeing nothing but a sea of gay men. He'd gotten used to dealing with families. Although it was nice not having to hide his sexuality in front of the guests, Griggs knew it was also dangerous.

Since hearing about the new direction the ranch was taking in dealing strictly with GLBT guests, Griggs had been counseling himself about getting involved with a guest. He knew it wasn't an option for him. He'd never been a one-night stand kind of guy. He preferred to take his time getting to know a potential lover. With only a week to maneuver, he knew "hands off" would have to become his motto.

As he climbed behind the wheel, Bridger reached out to take his cup.

"Here, let me hold that for you." Bridger grinned when their fingers brushed.

Griggs gave an inward groan. *Hands off.* He had to remember that.

Chapter Two

Although he had to share a room, Bridger was happy he'd been placed in what Griggs had called the summer cabin. He knew some guests had paid the premium for individual cabins, but the thought of spending the week alone in a cabin hadn't appealed to him.

He'd come to the Justice River Ranch for the chance to be himself for a change. Not only did he have to worry about his father's disapproving stares, but he could rope, ride and cuss at will.

"This okay with you?" Bridger asked his roommate, Steve, as he tossed his duffle onto one of the twin beds.

"Suits me," Steve answered.

Bridger unzipped his bag and began pulling out the small pile of clothes he'd brought. At the bottom of the duffle were his boots, wrapped in a plastic bag. He started to take them out of their container but stopped when he noticed all the dried mud at the bottom of the bag.

He set them aside and carried his clothes to the dresser. "I'll take the bottom drawer."

"Thanks." Steve, a financial planner, was probably in his mid to upper forties. Bridger didn't consider him heavy, but the older man did have a spare tire around his middle.

"Do you know if we're supposed to go ahead and change now, or are we doing that after supper?"

Steve stopped unloading his large suitcase, a huge pile of shirts in his hands. "I'm not sure. I know they said we'd be riding a bit after dinner though."

"Guess I'll go ahead then." Bridger took out a pair of his worn jeans and tossed them onto the bed. "Is it going to bother you if I change in here?"

"Not at all," Steve answered.

"Cool." Bridger unzipped his low-rise jeans and pushed them to the floor. He toed off his sneakers and stepped out of the jeans. When he reached for his riding jeans, he caught the open-jawed stare coming from his roommate.

Bridger shrugged as he pulled his pants on as quickly as possible. "Sorry."

Steve cleared his throat. "No. I'm sorry. Guess I've never seen a pair of underwear like that in real life."

Bridger chuckled as he stuffed his cock into his jeans and zipped up. Although technically a thong, Bridger's underwear was little more than a pouch for his cock with a couple of tiny strings attached. "Don't have much choice with the low-rise pants. It's either these or flash your underwear for everyone to see."

Steve shifted and turned back to his suitcase.

Bridger shrugged and retrieved his jeans from the floor. He smoothed out as many wrinkles as he could and put them in the drawer. After kicking his sneakers under the bed, he picked up the sack with his boots. "I'll be on the porch."

He remembered to grab his cigarettes and lighter from the top of the dresser before leaving the room. As he walked through the rustic living room, he glanced at the huge rock fireplace. Although it was probably too warm for a fire, maybe he'd try to talk his fellow houseguests into one later in the evening when the temperature cooled down.

Once on the porch, he lit up and took the boots out of their bag. Sock-footed, he stood at the end of the porch and banged the old boots together, knocking off even more dried mud and manure.

He took a seat in one of the freshly painted green Adirondack chairs and leaned back. As he looked out over the snowcapped mountains in the distance, he continued to enjoy his cigarette.

Who knew something as simple as being able to smoke without hiding it could be so incredibly satisfying?

The screen door opened and Rodney, he thought the guy's name was, came out to join him. "Glad to see I'm not the only one with this filthy habit."

Bridger chuckled and rested his head against the back of the chair. "I enjoy every moment of smoking."

"Yeah, me, too."

Rodney sat in a chair across from Bridger and lit a cigarette. "Think we'll be able to smoke while we ride?"

Bridger shook his head. "Too risky. Besides, I'm sure butts littering the ground isn't the look the ranch is going for. I think Deacon said something about smoking being relegated to our porches and behind the cookhouse."

"Oh well. Guess I'll have to get my fill in the mornings then."

"I brought a bunch of nicotine gum. I'll give you some. It's not as good as the real thing, but they should keep you from biting someone's head off as the day wears on."

"Thanks." Rodney took another drag of his cigarette. "So what was that good-looking guy from the other group talking to you about earlier?"

Bridger had to think back. The only man he could picture by Rodney's description wore a long black ponytail. "Griggs?"

Rodney chuckled. "No. The other one. The guy in the red sports shirt."

"Oh. James. Yeah, he wanted to know if I played."

"And?" Rodney prompted.

"I told him I wasn't really into random sex. But hey, if you're interested, go for it. Seemed like he was desperate to get a little action this week."

Rodney snorted. "Probably married."

"Probably."

After a few moments, Rodney continued. "Still, I might need to sit by him at supper."

Bridger shoved his cigarette butt into the bucket filled with sand and laughed. "I imagine there'll be a lot of hooking up this week."

"You think? I got the feeling from the brochure it was discouraged."

Bridger picked up one of his boots and eased his foot inside, holding it by the straps. "Well they can't very well encourage orgies now can they? We're grown men. They probably figure what they don't see isn't their business."

"You like Griggs, huh?"

Bridger shrugged, reaching for his other boot. "He's hot, but kind of an ass."

"Yeah, well, he was watching you pretty closely. I'd say you could get some of that if you played your cards right."

Geez. Did he come to a ranch or a gay spa? "I just want to spend my time doing what I love."

Rodney started to laugh. "That's just what I was talking about doing."

Bridger pulled his pants legs down over his boots and stood. "Think I'll head to the barn to check out the horses. Interested?"

"Oh, yeah, I'm interested, but not in horses at the moment."

Bridger chuckled and stepped off the porch. He knew Rodney's type, always interested in what he could get but Bridger didn't play those games.

The dirt-and-grass road that led to the barn was rutted, but at least it didn't look like it had rained recently. He dodged several of the deepest holes and soon cleared the trees.

From his vantage point, the ranch resembled the one he'd left earlier that morning. Although the buildings were older and smaller than the ones on Collinsford Downs, they served the same purposes.

Before reaching the barn, he passed a small field with a lone horse behind the fence. He detoured and crossed the grass to reach the wire fence. "Hey, boy."

Bridger reached out and began to pet the gorgeous bay mustang. The horse's nostrils flared momentarily as it jerked its head back.

"I'm not gonna hurt you, boy," Bridger spoke in a soothing tone. He could tell from the spooked behavior of the horse it wasn't used to being handled, but he'd always had a way with animals.

Before long, the stallion accepted Bridger's touch, even going as far as to nuzzle against his hand several times. "You like carrots? Nah, you seem more like an apple fella to me."

"Get away from him!"

Bridger glanced over his shoulder to see a red-faced Griggs striding toward him. He pulled his hand back. "Sorry. Didn't mean to overstep. Just getting friendly with the locals."

Griggs reached out and pulled Bridger by the arm until he was away from the fence. "Well, that old boy isn't friendly. He'd just as soon bite off your finger than look at you."

"We were fine. Despite what you think, I do know a little about horses."

Griggs snorted. "What, did Mummy and Daddy give you riding lessons before you came?"

How the hell did this asshole ever seem remotely attractive to me? Bridger jerked his arm out of Griggs' grasp and walked away. He took a left at the fork in the road, not ready to head to the barn.

Kicking the large chunks of gravel as he walked, Bridger didn't even realize where he was until he heard a voice. He looked up and came face to face with the two men who ran the place. "Hey."

"Going somewhere?" the smaller of the two asked.

Bridger shrugged. "Just needed to get away for a few minutes." It was then he noticed the large house tucked back into the trees. "I'm sorry. I didn't mean to trespass."

The smaller man shielded his eyes from the sun and looked up at the bigger cowboy. "I forgot my sunglasses. Will you wait for me?"

"As long as it takes."

Laughing, the smaller man started jogging back towards the house.

Left alone with the big guy, Bridger held out his hand. "I'm sorry, but I don't remember your name. I'm Bridger."

"Deacon." The man gestured toward the running man. "The absent-minded fella is my partner, Ray."

Bridger smiled. "I promise to remember this time."

"So, how come you're already in need of time to yourself?"

Despite loathing the man who talked down to him, Bridger wasn't the kind to squeal on anyone. "Just did. Enjoying the scenery."

Deacon stuffed his hands in his back pockets and rocked back on his heels. "Don't let Griggs get to you. He can be a surly sonofabitch, but he's damn good at his job."

"Surly's an understatement," he mumbled.

Deacon was still chuckling when Ray rejoined them. "What'd I miss?"

Deacon nodded toward Bridger. "Griggs has been working his charms on Bridger."

Ray smiled and clapped his hands together. "I knew it!"

The two men started laughing, completely losing Bridger. He assumed it was some kind of inside joke and kept his mouth shut.

They walked toward the fork in the road, this time taking the branch that led to the cookhouse.

"Are you thirsty?" Ray asked.

"I could use something."

"I'm gonna check on Black Jack," Deacon said, bending to give Ray a quick kiss.

"If that cut isn't any better, you should probably call Doc Morgan," Ray hollered after Deacon.

Deacon threw up a hand in acknowledgment but didn't turn around.

Ray shook his head. "Men."

Bridger couldn't agree more. He followed Ray up the steps and into the cookhouse.

"Coffee? Tea?"

"Is there any diet soda by chance?" Bridger asked.

"In the fridge. Help yourself." Ray poured a cup of coffee and took a seat at one of the long tables.

Bridger wandered into the kitchen. "Excuse me, ma'am. Ray said it would be okay if I got a diet soda?"

"Sure. Bottom shelf. There are also some homemade chocolate chip cookies in that tin on the counter."

"Thanks." Bridger grabbed a can and a couple of cookies before heading back into the dining room. He placed one of the cookies in front of Ray. "She said they were homemade."

Ray picked up the cookie and ate it in three bites. "Libby makes the best cookies, but don't tell Mother that."

"Your mother works here?" Bridger nibbled on his cookie, trying to make it last. It was something he'd done since he was a kid. His mom used to tease him, saying he ate like a bunny.

Ray got up and snagged the tin of cookies from the counter. "Mother's real name is Martha. Since most of the hands who work here either live far away from home or just don't get along with their folks, they've come to think of her as Mother."

"That's nice." He watched as Ray ate two more cookies.

"So what seems to be the problem with Griggs?"

Bridger finished off his treat and washed it down with a drink. "I don't know. I guess because I'm younger than he is, he seems to think it's okay to treat me like I'm stupid or something." He shrugged. "I've had my fill of his snide comments about my horsemanship abilities."

"You ride?"

Bridger nodded. "Since I was big enough to sit in the saddle. My father owns a place down south, just east of Austin."

"Well don't let him get to you. He's pretty protective of his horses. Until you prove to him that you really do know what the hell you're doing, he'll take it out on you."

"Take what out on me? I still don't know why he hates me so much."

With a grin on his face, Ray put the lid back on the tin. "He's attracted to you. I could tell the first time I saw him look your way. Griggs prides himself on being in control. I imagine you're disrupting some of that control and he doesn't like it."

"Really? Is that the reason he nearly yanked my arm off when he caught me petting the mustang down the road?"

Ray seemed shocked. "Satan's Spawn let you pet him?"

"You named a horse Satan's Spawn?"

"Nah. His real name is Harry. We just call him by the other name because of his temperament. He's never been broke. Griggs bought him for a hundred and twenty-five bucks from the government after they rounded a bunch of 'em up out west of here."

"Huh. Well, it seemed nice enough to me."

Ray refilled his coffee cup. "It might be an interesting bet as to which one, Griggs or Harry, could be tamed first."

*****

Griggs was sitting at the makeshift desk he'd set up in the corner of the tack room when he heard booted feet on the old wood plank floor.

"Griggs?" Deacon called.

"Back here."

Deacon appeared in the doorway and leaned a shoulder against the jamb. "What're you working on?"

Griggs held up the pad of paper. "Just trying to get an idea of what horses to have Neil pull out of the corral for later."

When Deacon continued to stand there, Griggs knew there was something else on his boss' mind. "What?"

"What's going on between you and Bridger?"

"Bridger? Nothing! Why? Did he say something?"

"Not exactly. Found him wandering the road. He looked like he'd lost his best friend."

Despite how bothersome he found the kid, he hated to hear about him being upset. Exactly why it bothered him, he refused to acknowledge. "I caught him petting Harry and yelled at him."

Deacon's brows shot up. "Seriously? Satan let him get that close?"

Griggs refused to remember his initial reaction when he'd first spotted Bridger that close to the feral Mustang. He turned back to his work, afraid of inadvertently broadcasting his emotions to Deacon.

"I'll try to go easier on him." The last thing he wanted was to get on Deacon's bad side because of his unwelcomed attraction to Bridger.

"Good. He seems like a nice guy. Maybe you should try to get to know him."

"Yeah, right. And just about the time I start to like him, he'll go back to his cushy life," Griggs mumbled.

"You'll have to let someone through that thick skin of yours eventually, Griggs. Take it from someone who knows. Life's a hell of a lot easier when there's someone standing beside you."

Griggs gripped the pencil in his hand as he heard Deacon walk away. He agreed with the ranch manager. The thought of a long-term partner appealed to him, maybe too much. A short-term fling would do nothing to get him to where he wanted to be.

Chapter Three

Bridger made a point to sit as far away from Griggs as possible during supper. He'd returned to the summer cabin long enough to give himself his shot, surprised to see most of the other guests sitting around the living room on their laptops, mumbling about their offices falling apart without them.

He still didn't understand why someone would pay a couple thousand dollars to take a vacation and then work, but to each his own, he reckoned.

The player from earlier took the chair across from him and Bridger almost groaned. Smarmy married men definitely weren't his style.

"Haven't changed your mind, have you?" James asked.

"Nope. Sorry." Bridger was relieved when Rodney took the seat beside Mr. Smarmy.

For the rest of the meal, he attempted to block out the sexual innuendos flying between the two men across the table from him. Instead, he concentrated on his supper. The chicken fried steak was some of the best he'd ever eaten and the mashed potatoes were, thankfully, not from a box.

After finishing what he could, he took his plate and scraped the few remaining scraps into the chicken feed bucket, set his plate in the provided bin and dropped his silverware into the plastic bucket of soapy dishwater.

Bridger made a point to pop his head into the kitchen. "Fantastic dinner, Libby. Thanks so much."

"You're welcome. I'm making up pies for after the evening ride if you're interested."

Bridger rubbed his flat, but full, stomach. "Depends on how much of this I can work off between now and then."

As he headed to the back porch, Bridger lit up a cigarette. He once again took in the breathtaking views. Collinsford Downs had green rolling hills, but it didn't hold a candle to the majestic mountains that seemed to surround Justice River.

The longer he stared at the scenery, the more he yearned to say to hell with his family and follow his dreams. The sound of the screen door banging shut startled him.

Bridger glanced over his shoulder before quickly resuming his original position. He heard the flick of Griggs' lighter. The distinct smell of a menthol cigarette seemed to envelop him in a cloud of gray smoke.

After several moments, Griggs spoke. "If you wanna show me how well you can ride, I'll go ahead and pull a horse for you."

Bridger was caught between doing just that and stomping his foot and retreating to the summer cabin. Why should he prove his abilities to...

His mouth went dry as Griggs bent over to put his half-smoked cigarette into the sand bucket. *Oh, shit.* Who was he kidding? He wanted that ass. He wanted to wrap his legs around that hard body and ride the man like a jockey.

"Well?" Griggs asked as he headed around the corner of the cookhouse toward the barn.

Maybe if he showed the head wrangler he knew what he was doing, the man would stop treating him like a city slicker. Bridger dropped his butt into the bucket and followed Griggs.

He reached the barn about ten paces behind Griggs. He saw a whiteboard with guests' names matched up with horses' names. According to the list, Bridger was supposed to ride Jigsaw.

"If you'll point him out to me, I can go out into the corral and get my horse."

"I'll do that. Wouldn't want you to ruin your fancy sneakers."

Bridger cleared his throat. Griggs eventually turned away from the board and looked at him. Bridger pointed down to his worn boots. For some reason it hurt that Griggs hadn't even paid enough attention to him to notice the boots he'd worn all afternoon and evening. "They've seen their share of muddy corrals. I'll be fine."

Griggs continued to stare at Bridger's boots for several moments before slowly working his gaze up.

Bridger felt the look like a physical touch. When Griggs' eyes zeroed in on Bridger's groin, he felt himself start to harden. The wicked grin of Griggs' sensual mouth told Bridger the wrangler had noticed his predicament.

"Black and white gelding." Griggs tossed Bridger a lead rope. "I've already haltered him."

Bridger caught the red and white nylon rope and nodded. He spun on his heels and walked down the steep ramp at one end of the barn into the corral. In a sea of dun and roan horseflesh, the black and white was easy to find.

"Hey, Jigsaw," Bridger cooed. He snapped the lead onto the horse's halter and immediately began to pet the gorgeous animal.

A large, steel gray horse caught his eye as it walked toward him. "Well aren't you a beauty." He reached out and stroked the big gray's forehead and neck.

"He's mine," Griggs said from behind Bridger.

"He's gorgeous. What's his name?" Bridger removed his hand, afraid of being yelled at.

"Mick," Griggs answered. Instead of attaching the lead, Griggs whistled and headed back toward the barn, Mick following the large man like a puppy.

Bridger smiled. He couldn't imagine anything, horse or man, being able to resist Griggs' deep voice and commanding attitude. Hell, he'd follow that ass himself if Griggs would let him.

He led Jigsaw out of the corral to the hitching post. After a quick tie down, Bridger wandered into the tack room. "Is there a specific saddle Jigsaw prefers?"

Griggs came out of a small room off to the side carrying a black saddle and blanket. "He doesn't like the weight of most saddles, so I usually use number six with the black and red checked blanket."

Bridger nodded. He walked down the aisle of sawhorses until he came to one marked with a big red six on the floor in front of it. Like Griggs had indicated, the saddle was extremely light. Bridger wondered how Jigsaw felt about having a hundred-and-fifty pound man on his back.

He carried the saddle over to the row of blankets draped over a pole running down the center of the room. He found the black and red and set the saddle on top before picking them both up as one unit.

Griggs was cinching his saddle when Bridger exited the barn.

"You got it?" Griggs asked.

"Yeah." Bridger wasted no time getting Jigsaw saddled. "Bridle?"

With his back leaning against Mick, Griggs had his arms crossed. "Number eleven."

Voices erupted from the cookhouse as the guests poured out onto the porch and down the steps.

"Would you like me to help them with their horses?" Bridger asked.

Griggs hadn't moved a muscle. He continued to study Bridger, but finally gave a slow nod. "Yeah. I'd appreciate that."

Before helping the other men, Bridger found the right bridle and finished off Jigsaw. He spent the next hour working beside Griggs and the other wranglers, teaching the guests how to saddle their horses.

Once he helped get the last guest mounted, Bridger untied Jigsaw's reins from the hitching post and swung himself into the saddle. He felt eyes on him and turned to find Griggs, once again, staring at him.

Bridger stared back this time. Although he knew Griggs would never say the words, he could tell the man was starting to regret some of his snide comments.

Griggs broke eye contact and addressed the group. "Nothing too strenuous this evening. We'll ride up the road about a mile before turning back. I'll use the time to judge your fit with the horse I've assigned. If you're having trouble with your mount, let me know and we'll try a different one next time."

Bridger hung back, content watching Griggs interact with the other guests. Despite the head wrangler's surly attitude towards him, the man was surprisingly patient with the inexperienced riders.

"You look good. I take it you've done this before," Cody said, riding up beside Bridger.

Bridger chuckled. "Yeah. I ride as often as I'm allowed. Usually when my father's out of town."

Bridger snapped his mouth shut. He'd almost told too much to a stranger. All he'd hoped for was a week of being Bridger Collins instead of his father's son. Instead of questioning him further, Cody got sidetracked by a yelp from one of the men whose horse wasn't cooperating.

"Sorry." Cody rode off toward the man.

Bridger's attention returned to the scenery, in particular the setting sun. The bright hues of red and orange painted not only the mountains, but the entire landscape. This was how he wanted to spend his days. Not trapped in a high-rise in Austin.

By the time they returned to the barn, Bridger was pissed. Not with Griggs. The anger fueling his blood was directed at two people, himself and his father. He unsaddled Jigsaw and brushed him down.

Once he finished, Bridger knew he should help the others, but he didn't feel like it. Instead of getting a lead rope, he hooked a finger through Jigsaw's halter and led his mount out toward the open field. Bridger gave the black-and-white paint one last nuzzle before releasing him. "You done good, boy."

He was surprised when Jigsaw didn't run for the hills. Instead the horse stood where he was, bumping his forehead against Bridger's shoulder. Bridger walked along the fence, leading the paint away from the gate.

In the clear, away from the other horses, Bridger climbed onto the slat-board fence and continued to pet and scratch Jigsaw behind the ears.

"Why can't I be man enough to defy him?" Bridger asked the animal.

He wasn't sure how long he sat there before Griggs' horse Mick trotted by.

"Everyone's in the cookhouse having pie. If you want some, you'd better get in there," Griggs said, closing the pasture gate.

Jigsaw started to wander off toward the big gray and Bridger climbed down from his perch. He watched as his horse met up with Mick before turning to reply to Griggs. "Not really in the mood for pie."

"Thanks for your help," Griggs mumbled.

Bridger wondered how much the gratitude had cost the wrangler. He waited until the horses had disappeared into the darkness before turning toward Griggs. "No problem."

He walked past Griggs and headed to the barn, halter in hand. After hanging the bright red halter with the others, he pulled the elastic ponytail holder out of his hair and shook his head.

"Listen. I'm sorry I was so hard on you earlier. There've been a lot of people come here that claim to know how to ride only to end up dumped on their ass the first time we go off road. I can tell by your seat you know what you're doing," Griggs acknowledged.

Bridger leaned against one of the barn support beams and crossed his arms. "I grew up on my father's ranch in Texas."

Griggs tilted his hat up with the tip of his finger. "Yeah?" He nodded. "Makes sense. You look right at home in a barn."

Bridger snorted. "Don't let my ease fool you. There's a reason why a man who grew up on a ranch would willingly pay to spend his vacation on someone else's."

Griggs took several steps toward Bridger. "Why are you here?"

Moving his hands to his hips, Bridger glanced around the dimly lit barn. "Because at home I have to hide who I am. I wanted the chance to feel free."

Griggs stepped even closer. "Your folks don't know you're gay?"

Bridger chuckled. "It's kind of obvious isn't it?" He shook his head. "No. I came out to them when I was fifteen."

Griggs reached out and ran a hand over Bridger's hair, slipping underneath to grasp the back of his neck. "Then what are you hiding?"

"My desire to work cattle, ride horses…" Bridger shrugged. "As the song goes, I wanna be a cowboy."

Griggs pressed his body against Bridger's. "Your dad owns a ranch. That should be a no-brainer."

Bridger couldn't help himself. Despite what had happened between them earlier in the day, he still wanted the six-foot-two wrangler. He stood on his tiptoes and tilted his chin up.

"No more talk about my father. Kiss me," he whispered against Griggs' lips.

The press of the cowboy's mouth against his was soft at first. Bridger felt the tip of Griggs' tongue and opened immediately, sucking the tender flesh inside.

Griggs groaned and tilted his head, taking the kiss even deeper. The gentle flicks and swirls of Griggs' tongue drove Bridger wild. He ground his hardened cock against the strong thigh nestled between his legs as he continued to fall deeper and deeper into the kiss. Bridger wanted it all. He wanted to be consumed by the man kissing him.

The hand on his neck disappeared and Griggs was soon lifting Bridger off his feet. Caught between the beam at his back and the muscled chest in front of him, Bridger wrapped his legs around Griggs' hips. The crush of Griggs' body against his hard cock would be enough to make him come, but he wanted so much more. Bridger wiggled as much as the new position allowed, hoping like hell he could turn Griggs on as much as he was.

Griggs was the first to break the kiss. He stared into Bridger's eyes. "God help me, but I want you."

Bridger nodded his agreement, too turned on by Griggs apparent need to verbalize his desires. He felt large hands knead his butt as Griggs began to grind against him. He worked a hand between them and cupped the large cock that continued to torture him. Fat and long, Griggs' cock felt perfect in his hand. Bridger wondered if he could open his mouth wide enough to accommodate its incredible size. "Let me taste you."

Fire sparked in Griggs' eyes as he lowered Bridger to the floor.

With shaking hands, Bridger unfastened the top snap of Griggs' jeans before easing the zipper down. He wanted to please Griggs enough to have him begging for more. After separating the denim, he slipped his fingers under the elastic of Griggs' underwear. Goose flesh broke out on his skin as his anticipation increased. Sparse pubic hair tickled his palm moments before he wrapped his hand around his prize.

Griggs moaned. "Suck me."

Bridger removed his hand and sank to his knees, pulling Griggs' clothing down with him. The heavily veined cock that sprang free took his breath away. He was in no way a virgin, but his limited experience had him questioning his ability to please a man of Griggs' size.

Griggs grabbed his shaft by the base and rubbed it across Bridger's cheek, slapping the heavy erection against Bridger's flesh, painting Bridger's lips with drops of pre-cum. The gesture almost felt to Bridger like he was being marked, branded in some erotic show of dominance. Although he'd never had the desire to be dominated in sexual play, he quickly discovered just how much it turned him on.

Bridger looked up into Griggs' black eyes as he opened his mouth and stuck out his tongue. The feel of the bulbous head tapping against his tongue was hotter than hell.

As he closed his lips over the crown, he reached down and opened his own jeans. Bridger shoved his hand down his pants and gripped the base of his cock, afraid he'd show his inexperience and come prematurely. The first moment he tasted Griggs' pre-cum, he knew he'd forever be addicted. The flavorful liquid coated his tongue as he took the cock as deep as he could.

Even though it was evident Griggs enjoyed being in charge, he didn't force more down Bridger's throat than he thought he could take. Bridger wished he'd learned to deep throat a lover, but Griggs didn't seem to mind. Instead, Bridger concentrated on jacking Griggs' cock with both hands while he sucked and slurped his way around the large head and a few inches of length.

With a deep groan, Griggs buried his fingers deeper in Bridger's hair and began a shallow thrust in and out of Bridger's mouth.

Bridger released the base of his cock and pushed the pouch of his underwear under his balls. For the first time, he indulged in the length of his own erection, sliding his hand up and down its length while he continued to pleasure Griggs with his mouth. The cavernous barn echoed with the sounds of their mutual lust. Griggs reached down and knocked Bridger's hand away from his cock in yet another display of dominance. Bridger settled on playing with the heavy sac that hung below Griggs' shaft.

"I'm gonna come. Pull off or prepare yourself," Griggs warned.

Bridger pulled his head back enough to taste and swallow. With a howl from Griggs, the first splash of seed landed on his taste buds. Before he could fully appreciate the rich flavor, his mouth was flooded by strings of cum. He felt a bit of overflow start to dribble down his chin, but he was too busy swallowing to do anything about it.

After nursing the cock clean, Bridger got to his feet and pressed his exposed dick against Griggs. The bigger man groaned and licked the errant cum from Bridger's chin as he took over the job of manipulating Bridger's erection.

"Will you come for me?"

At that moment, Bridger knew he'd do anything the man wanted. When Griggs' calloused thumb pressed against the sensitive underside of Bridger's cock, he lost every ounce of his control. He filled Griggs' hand with cum as he shook with desire.

If Griggs hadn't been holding him, Bridger knew he would've fallen to the ground. It had been one of the most trying days of his life, both emotionally and sexually and he wasn't ready for it to end.

He continued to cling to Griggs' chest, words of need on the tip of his tongue. He wondered how often the wrangler had seduced a guest of the ranch. Was he just one of many?

Bridger rubbed his cheek against Griggs' collarbone, content to stay in the man's arms for the rest of his vacation.

He heard the sounds of Griggs licking the cum from his hand. "I'll walk you back to your cabin."

Bridger stepped back and began the process of redressing himself. For some reason he couldn't look at the man he'd just had his most erotic experience with.

He was trying to adjust the pouch of his underwear when Griggs stopped him by tilting his chin up. "Thank you."

Bridger nodded, but kept his mouth shut, afraid he'd say something he'd later regret.

"It's too soon," was the only explanation Griggs gave him.

Bridger continued to dress as he tried to figure out what the statement meant. Was Griggs saying there was a possibility for more later? How much later?

Griggs hand landed on the small of Bridger's back. "Come on."

He made the tour of the barn as Griggs turned off the overhead lights. When they stepped out into the night, Bridger was surprised at how chilly it had become. Gooseflesh broke across his skin as he took a chance and huddled closer to Griggs' side.

"It'll be even colder in the morning, so make sure you wear a jacket or a sweatshirt. You'll want it to be something warm, but easy to tie around your waist as the day heats up."

After a few hundred yards, Griggs stopped and turned Bridger to face the east. "See the small house with the porch light on?"

"Yeah."

"That's mine."

Bridger gazed up into Griggs' perfectly chiseled face. "Is that an invitation?"

"Not yet, but soon." Griggs leaned down and pressed a kiss to Bridger's lips. "Real soon."

Chapter Four

ಸ

With a coffee cup in one hand and a cigarette in the other, Griggs sat on his front porch and watched Neil and his Australian Shepherd, Georgia, run the horses over the hill and down into the corral.

It was his favorite part of the day. The reason he'd long ago decided to make the ranch his home. There was just something about the majestic seen of horse and rider working against the backdrop of the rising sun that never ceased to take his breath away.

He heard the scrape of boots on dirt and smiled as he got his first look of the day of another breathtaking sight. With his black curls tamed into a low-riding ponytail, Bridger stepped up onto the porch.

"Morning."

Griggs put his cigarette out and patted the swing beside him. "How'd you sleep?"

Bridger yawned as he settled against Griggs' side. "Shitty. You guys should put snorers in some kind of soundproof room."

"Your roommate?"

Bridger nodded. "I ended up crawling to the couch around three o'clock."

Griggs passed Bridger his coffee cup. "Maybe this'll wake you up."

Bridger took a sip. "Mmm."

Bridger's moan over the fresh brew reminded Griggs of the previous night. He'd also gotten very little sleep but it had nothing to do with a snoring man sleeping beside him.

With his lover's hands wrapped around the ceramic mug for warmth, Griggs leaned down and kissed him, thrusting his tongue in to taste coffee, cigarettes and Bridger.

He knew he needed to head to the barn to harness the horses, but he couldn't bring himself to remove his lips from Bridger's. A perfect morning had been made even more perfect with the addition of the sexy man beside him. What would it be like to share his normal sunrise ritual with Bridger every morning?

Griggs shook off the thought before he started building dreams that couldn't come true. "If we hurry, I bet we have time for a short ride before they ring the breakfast bell," he informed Bridger.

Bridger took another sip of coffee before passing the cup back to Griggs. "That sounds nice."

The cup was set on the small table beside the swing and Griggs stood. He pulled Bridger up and into his arms. "You know you never finished your story last night."

"I know. Maybe the ride will help loosen my tongue."

Griggs brushed his lips across Bridger's. "Or maybe I can do it some other way."

Just like every time he'd kissed the younger man, his passion threatened to overwhelm him. He broke away and shook his head. "You're trouble."

Bridger grinned, twin dimples looking as sexy as they ever had. "Me? Nah. I'm just a simple country boy."

* * * * *

Bridger couldn't keep his eyes off Griggs as they rode toward a bluff. Once again he was on Jigsaw. After that first ride, Bridger couldn't imagine being on any other horse.

"So, is your tongue loose enough yet?" Griggs asked, pulling Mick closer to Jigsaw.

"I told you my father owned a ranch, but he's not exactly what you'd call a rancher. He's strictly a businessman, a rich, self-centered, pompous ass who oversees the bottom line of the ranch. In his opinion, we're too good to actually do the manual work involved. I was allowed to ride growing up, but it wasn't unless my father was on a business trip that I could sneak and actually work with the other hands."

"Well you're not a kid anymore. Have you told him what you want?"

Bridger snorted. "You don't *tell* Theodore Collinsford anything."

"Collinsford? You mean...?"

"Yeah. That Collinsford. I didn't put my real last name on the registration form. I just wanted to be Bridger Collins, even if for only a week."

Theodore Collinsford was one of the richest men in the country. The ranch Bridger had grown up on was the symbol of the Collinsford empire, but the heart of the company was the hundreds of Collinsford feed lots and farm stores sprinkled around the country. It seemed every decent-sized town had a Collinsford Farm Supply store where customers could buy everything from hardware items, tools and lumber to feed and seed.

Griggs rode closer, reaching out to brush a hand across Bridger's back. "I take it your dad wants you to work the business side of the company."

"Yeah. I'm forced to do the nine-to-five thing on school breaks. God, I hate it."

They reached the top of the bluff and Bridger walked Jigsaw as close to the edge as was prudent. He gazed out over the ranch buildings below. They reminded him of the toys he played with as a child.

"I feel like every day I spend inside that damn glass building, a small piece of my soul shrivels." He turned his head to look at Griggs. "I love my mom and if I were really pressed, I'd admit to loving my father as well, but I can't do what I want and not walk away from both of them. My father has made that much perfectly clear."

Bridger started to fold in on himself. "I just wish I was a stronger person."

In a matter of seconds, Griggs had dismounted and pulled Bridger off Jigsaw and into his arms. "No one should have to choose between their family and the life they want to lead."

Bridger held onto Griggs with all his might. He wished he could be as sure of himself as Griggs was. "It's not the money. I don't care anything about it. It's…"

"Shhh," Griggs soothed, burying his face in Bridger's hair. "I know you signed up for the full ranch experience. Why don't we make sure you get just that? At least it'll give you a better idea if this is what you want to do for the rest of your life."

Bridger nodded, willing himself not to cry. No way would a strong man like Griggs be impressed with a fucking crybaby. "Does that mean I can go out with Neil instead of hanging around with the other guests?"

Griggs' arms tightened. "As long as you come find me at the end of the day."

Bridger looked up and grinned. "I'll seek you out at every opportunity if you let me."

Griggs ran his hands over Bridger's ass, stopping to squeeze his cheeks. "Tonight's the big dinner in the Justice side of the summer cabin. I have to help grill, but I'd love to take you as my date."

"What time is that?"

"Seven."

"I'll make sure I'm done in time." Bridger pulled Griggs' head down for a kiss. He wished they could crawl into bed and forget about doing anything but making love the rest of the day.

He felt Griggs' hard cock rub against him and moaned, breaking the kiss. "You keep that up and I'll be following you around like a pet for the rest of the week."

Griggs ran his knuckle up and down Bridger's cheek. "Something tells me I might not mind."

* * * * *

After an entire day of rounding up stray cattle and fixing fences, Bridger was completely worn out, but it was a damn good feeling.

By the time he took care of Jigsaw and released him into the pasture, it was nearing seven. Drawing on the last of his energy, Bridger jogged back to the guests' side of the summer cabin. The rest of his housemates were already showered, dressed and sitting on the porch drinking beer.

"Where've you been?" Steve asked.

"Working with Neil. I'm just gonna jump in the shower real quick. If Griggs is looking for me, tell him I'll be right out."

"Griggs?" Rodney grinned. "You lucky sonofabitch."

Bridger grinned and ran into the house. He grabbed a clean pair of underwear, the jeans he'd worn to fly in and a red button-down shirt before entering the bathroom. He laid his clean clothes out on the vanity and dug underneath the sink for the shaving kit he'd stashed there earlier that morning.

As he brushed his teeth, he ran his electric razor over his cheeks and neck, killing two birds with one stone. The shower was just as quick, although he took special care in soaping all his nooks and crannies.

By the time he stepped out of the shower and dried off, he was hard, which wouldn't have been a problem except the underwear and the low-rise jeans didn't lend themselves to such a condition.

Instead of tucking in his shirt, he decided to leave the tails free to hide his obvious erection. Hopefully he'd get a chance to sneak away with Griggs and take care of it. He slapped on a little of his favorite aftershave and gathered his dirty clothes, dirty being a huge understatement.

Bridger tossed his clothes onto his bed, stuck his cigarettes and lighter into his shirt pocket and grabbed a beer out of the fridge. He arrived back on the porch with about three minutes to spare.

"Damn, that was fast," Rodney commented.

Bridger leaned against one of the porch supports and lit a cigarette. It was his first one since lunch and he'd forgotten to take his nicotine gum with him. He felt his head begin to swim as the nicotine hit his system.

The screen door of the Justice side of the summer cabin opened and Deacon and Ray appeared. "Anyone hungry?"

Not finished with his cigarette, Bridger held back as the fifteen other guests entered the house.

When the last of them were in, Bridger walked over to the butt bucket and sank his cigarette into the sand.

"There you are," a deep, sexy voice said from behind him.

When Bridger stood, spots peppered his vision. He rocked back slightly on his heels, trying to get his bearings.

"Hey." Griggs' strong arms wrapped around Bridger's waist and turned him around. "You okay?"

Bridger blinked several times before nodding. "I think it's the combination of going too long without a cigarette, bending over and being late for my shot."

Griggs' black eyes narrowed. "Do you always mess around with your diabetes this way?"

Bridger felt worse than he'd dare let on. "No, but then again, I usually live such a boring routine, it's hard to forget." He ran his hands over Griggs' western-style dress shirt. "You fill my head to the point I can't think of anything else."

Griggs led Bridger over to one of the Adirondack chairs. "Sit."

Bridger felt too shaky to argue. "My kit's on top of my dresser."

Griggs disappeared into the house, returning moments later with Bridger's black leather bag and a small plastic bottle of orange juice from the refrigerator.

Bridger was starting to sweat, despite the cool evening. He reached for the kit, but Griggs shook his head.

"This first." Griggs opened the juice and held it to Bridger's lips.

He drank about half of the bottle before nodding that he'd had enough. "Give me a second."

"I'll be right back." Griggs ran across the porch into the Justice side of the summer cabin.

While Bridger waited for the juice to raise his blood sugar levels, he started fumbling with the kit, trying to get out the needed supplies.

"I'll do it," Griggs said, handing Bridger a slice of American cheese.

Bridger was surprised but in no condition to argue. He knew it was a combination of a change in his daily activity level and not eating on time. Like a pro, Griggs pulled out the lancet and pricked Bridger's middle finger. After several firm squeezes, he dabbed the blood onto one of the test strips.

Bridger checked his blood sugar reading and adjusted his pen accordingly. He was fumbling with his zipper when Griggs took over the job of getting Bridger's pants down. "Is this set to the correct dose?"

Bridger nodded. He was so accustomed to the injections, he didn't even feel it.

Griggs began putting the supplies back into the kit bag. "Any better?"

Bridger nodded again, wiping the sweat from his forehead. He wasn't sure how long he sat there before he felt he was finally coherent enough to talk. Although he felt incredibly stupid, he was also curious. "How'd you know?"

"My sister Rachel." Griggs sat back on his ass and shook his head. "You've got to get a handle on this thing."

"I know. I think my body isn't used to the ass kicking Neil shelled out earlier. Like I told you, my life is incredibly routine at home. I just didn't take into account the change in my normal activity level."

"Do you need to go to a doctor?"

"No. I need to sit here for a few more minutes and then I need to eat." He reached out and tugged on Griggs' ponytail. "Thank you."

Griggs leaned forward and rested his forehead on Bridger's lap. "You scared me."

"I know. I'm sorry."

"Don't do it again, okay?"

Bridger released Griggs' hair from the leather tie and ran his fingers through it. "I'll be a good boy. I promise."

Griggs turned his head and kissed Bridger's inner thigh where he'd evidently given the injection. "Not too good, just good enough to keep yourself alive for all the bad things I want to do with you."

"Deal."

* * * * *

After getting Bridger's jeans pulled up and zipped, Griggs led him into the party. Most of the guests were seated at the extra long table enjoying red wine and appetizers. He pulled out a chair and made sure his lover was comfortable. He put a hand on Bridger's shoulder and whispered in his ear.

"There's water on the table, or would you prefer something else?"

"Water's fine," Bridger said, reaching up to put his hand over Griggs'.

Griggs brought Bridger's water glass closer before retreating to the kitchen. He was tying his hair back as he caught up with the rest of the staff. "Sorry to run out on you like that."

"Bridger okay?" Ray asked.

"Yeah." Griggs looked at Neil. "Someone worked him too hard today and kept him out too long."

Neil chuckled. "Me? You've got that backwards. Bridger was the one who insisted on checking that last pasture, not me."

Griggs started to argue, but stopped himself. "Yeah. That sounds like him. Regardless, from now on, if he goes out to work with you, make sure he stops a couple of times and eats something. It might not be a bad idea to grab one of those saddle bags out of the tack room and make him take his insulin kit with him along with a couple of extra water bottles."

Neil nodded. "Not a problem. He's good help and damn, can he ride."

Griggs felt himself puff with a bit of pride at the compliment.

Deacon came in the back door. "Steaks are almost done. You might go ahead and serve the salads."

Griggs pulled out one of the large trays and started filling it with the already-made plates of salad. "Grab that pitcher of water, Cody."

Tray in hand, he pushed through the swinging door and almost dropped the entire load of food. His face pale, Bridger was shaking his head as James whispered in his ear. "What're you doing?"

James released Bridger's arm and smiled. "Just talking."

Griggs had to pull his temper back quickly before he exploded. "Take your seat. We're serving dinner."

With an overly confident smirk on his face, James settled into the chair beside Bridger.

"Griggs is sitting there," Bridger informed the older man.

"Looks to me like he's playing waiter," James answered.

With as much calm as he could muster, Griggs set the tray on the table and stalked toward James.

"Griggs. No." Bridger stood and put a hand on Griggs' chest. "He's not worth it."

Griggs stared over Bridger's shoulder at the man in question. "No, but you are."

"I'm fine. I just really, really need to eat something."

Griggs looked down at Bridger. "Follow me."

He reached out and took Bridger's hand and led him into the kitchen. "Cody, will you serve the salads? If I do it, one of our guests will probably not only end up wearing his but taking a trip to the emergency room in Red Lodge."

He pulled out one of the stools at the black granite island. "Have a seat."

Deciding it would be better if he kept out of the dining room, Griggs fixed another big glass of ice water and set it in front of Bridger. "I'll get your steak."

"You don't have to do this. I can handle guys like James."

Griggs leaned over and kissed him. "Sit tight."

Grabbing a plate from the cupboard, he went outside where Deacon was loading steaks onto a platter. "One please."

Deacon's brows shot up. "Hungry?"

"It's for Bridger. He's getting too much unwanted attention from one of the guests. I've got him in the kitchen."

Deacon used a pair of tongs to take a perfectly cooked steak off the grill and slide it onto the plate. "I understand that you like Bridger, but don't forget we're trying to run a business."

"I know. Which is why the guy's still breathing." He took the plate into the kitchen and set it in front of Bridger. He spooned some roasted potatoes and green beans onto the plate. "Anything else?"

Bridger shook his head and began cutting into the meat. "Don't get into trouble because of me."

Griggs buried his fingers in Bridger's curls and kissed the top of his head. "You concentrate on eating and I'll finish doing my job like a good wrangler."

As he helped Deacon, Cody and Ray get the plates filled, he couldn't keep from glancing at Bridger every few moments. The younger man's color was back to normal by the time he'd taken several bites of steak and potatoes.

"Do I need to eat in the dining room?" he asked Ray.

"No, that's okay. Just help us carry the plates out and you can come back in here." Ray leaned closer. "I've overheard James a time or two, so I don't blame you. If he'd fixed his sights on Deacon, he'd be walking his way back to Billings about now."

Griggs smiled. He'd only known Ray for about seven months, but he already thought of him as a good friend. "Thanks."

Ray slapped him on the back. "As a matter of fact, if you wanted to volunteer to wash that sink full of pots and pans, I might be persuaded to let you just stay in here."

"I can do that." Griggs started some hot, soapy water in the sink and filled his plate.

"Sorry I screwed up our date," Bridger mumbled around a bite of food.

"You haven't ruined anything. If you feel up to it, I thought maybe we could grab your duffle and head over to my place when we're finished."

Bridger's eyes rounded in apparent surprise. "My duffle?"

Griggs turned off the water and dried his hands. "You need your sleep and I think it's obvious after last night you're not going to get it sharing a room with Steve."

Bridger took another bite of his potatoes. Griggs couldn't tell what was going on in his lover's head, but he knew Bridger was thinking about something important.

"James isn't in the summer cabin, ya know."

Oh. So Bridger thought Griggs was asking out of jealousy instead of want. "I know that. I'd planned on asking you before any of this happened."

"You did?"

"Yeah. I mean, it makes sense and that way I can keep a better eye on you."

Bridger rolled his eyes. "Seriously, I'm not as lame as I may appear. I really can take care of my body."

"Really? So what about the smoking? Do you realize how bad that is for you?"

Bridger put down his fork and reached out his hand. "Hello, Mr. Pot, I'm Mr. Kettle."

Griggs blew out a frustrated breath. "Number one, I'm not a diabetic. Number two, before you showed up, I really didn't care if I died a couple years sooner and number three…"

Bridger shut Griggs up with a kiss. "I'll quit if you will."

"In the next week?"

Bridger shook his head and pushed his plate away. "I keep forgetting."

So do I. Griggs swallowed around the lump in his throat.

Chapter Five
෨

Griggs rubbed against the warm body spooned to his front. He opened his eyes and glanced at the clock on the bedside table before returning his attention to the naked man in his arms.

Events of the previous evening were still forefront in his mind. He'd dealt with Bridger's diabetic episode and his jealousy toward one of the guests, but those things weren't what bothered him the most.

By the time they'd returned to his house, Bridger barely had the strength to undress and crawl into bed. Griggs had given Bridger a few kisses before wrapping his lover in his arms and ordering him to sleep.

He'd spent the entire night with a man and hadn't done a damn thing. What bothered him the most was that he was okay with the outcome. It wasn't that he didn't want to make love with the gorgeous younger man, but he felt satisfied to simply hold him. The frightening part was he knew what it meant.

I'm falling for him. Even the idea scared the shit out of him. He'd tried so hard to convince himself it was a purely physical attraction that had drawn him to Bridger. The first time he'd laid eyes on the man, he'd wanted him. Now he knew it was more than that. He'd pushed Bridger away because something told him the younger man had the ability to burrow under his skin.

Griggs' thumb brushed across Bridger's nipple as he tried to figure out what to do. He'd only known Bridger for two days. He was standing at a crossroads. The decision was his.

Should he back off and save what was left of his heart, or spend each day like it was their last?

Bridger's ass wiggled, pushing further back against Griggs' morning wood. The feel of his cock nestled against Bridger's warmth went a long way in helping him decide. Emotions aside, Bridger still was one of the sexiest men he'd ever known.

He ran his hand down Bridger's chest to the short nest of curls. Bridger's cock jumped at the subtle touch.

"You awake?" a sleepy voice mumbled.

"Yeah. I get up at this time every day. I didn't mean to wake you. I just couldn't help myself."

Bridger reached back and spread the cheeks of his ass, further enveloping Griggs' cock in the cleft. "You've got a nice bed."

"Seems a hell of a lot nicer with you in it." He removed his hand from Bridger's body and blindly reached behind him. Before getting into bed the previous evening, he'd set out condoms and lube. He grabbed both, nearly knocking the lamp over in his haste.

Bridger chuckled at Griggs' fumbling. "In a hurry?"

"Something like that." Griggs rolled to his back, pulling his other arm free. He popped the top on the small bottle of lube and slicked his fingers before resuming his original position. "Am I moving too fast?"

Bridger thrust his ass toward Griggs. "Touch me."

At the age of thirty-six, Griggs had fucked his share of men, but the first brush of his lubed finger against the tight pucker of Bridger's ass threatened his control. It wasn't that he'd never had feelings for another lover, but usually the physical side of the relationship developed before his emotions started to kick in.

He swirled the pad of his finger around the soft ridges, waiting for the muscles to relax. Griggs kissed the bare shoulder in front of him and slipped the tip of his finger inside Bridger's hole.

"Mmm." Bridger twisted his head to the side, making his lips accessible.

Griggs wasted no time. He sealed his mouth over Bridger's and plunged his finger inside the tight heat of his lover's body. As Bridger sucked on his tongue, Griggs continued to stretch the younger man's hole.

"Need you," Bridger whispered.

Griggs withdrew his fingers and rolled them until he was on top. He braced his hands against the bed and rose up to look down at his lover. As he stared into Bridger's dark grey eyes he smiled. "I knew they'd change colors."

"Huh?"

"Your eyes. They look like a stormy Montana sky."

"How poetic of you," Bridger said around a chuckle.

"Guess I'm feeling rather poetic at the moment." He leaned down and kissed the soft lips that continued to mesmerize him.

"I don't want to le—" Bridger cut himself off.

"You don't want to what?"

Several moments went by before Bridger answered. "I don't want to leave this bed."

Griggs stared into Bridger's eyes, trying to figure out if his lover was telling the truth. He'd hoped to hear something different, but he'd take what he could get. "I'm not shoving you out. That's for damn sure."

He reached for the condom package and ripped it open. Although their lust had cooled slightly, he knew it wouldn't take long to heat up again and this time he wanted to be ready.

After sheathing his cock, Griggs returned his attention to Bridger's mouth. Bridger truly was the best kisser he'd ever met. Just as he'd predicted, the passion between them began to build as Bridger sucked on his tongue.

Without breaking their kiss, Griggs squirted more lube onto his fingers and reached between their bodies. He eased three fingers into Bridger's hole and applied more slick. The last thing he wanted was to hurt his new lover.

"Fuck me," Bridger begged.

Griggs removed his fingers, wiping the excess lube onto the condom and directed the head of his cock to Bridger's stretched opening.

With a deep groan, Griggs slowly drove his cock inside. He felt Bridger's short nails scrape the skin of his back, which only heightened the experience.

"Oh, shit. Oh, shit," Bridger continued to chant as Griggs began to fuck him. Bridger hooked his legs over Griggs' shoulders and began to buck his body back and forth on Griggs' shaft.

His lover's enthusiasm was contagious and soon Griggs was pounding Bridger's tight ass with everything he had. Gooseflesh covered his body as he fought to stave off his climax.

Without even touching his cock, Bridger came, splashing warm seed over both of them.

"Fuck!" Griggs howled as his balls drew up and filled the condom with his cum. He dropped down on top of Bridger as the aftershocks continued to wrack his body with shudders.

He burrowed under his lover's hair and found Bridger's neck. He kissed the sweaty skin before latching on to bring up a dark bruise. He hoped every time James saw the bruise he'd be reminded that Bridger was already taken. Because in Griggs' mind, Bridger was most definitely his.

*****

Plate in hand, Bridger sat in the chair Griggs had obviously saved for him. "Hey."

Griggs set down his glass of iced tea. "How's your day going?"

"Good. We checked the fencing in Abigail's Valley earlier. Neil decided we should replace one of the hinges on the gate, so we'll do that after lunch."

Bridger couldn't believe it was Thursday already. He was supposed to head back to Billings on Saturday afternoon, but he'd been doing some heavy thinking all day. Neil had mentioned while they were out that he should ask Ray and Deacon for a job.

He wanted to jump at the opportunity, but two very important things held him back. First and foremost, was his budding relationship with Griggs. Bridger knew he'd be devastated if he found out Griggs was only interested in a short-term fling. The other problem, of course, was telling his parents. Regardless, he knew it would be something he'd have to take care of in person.

"What's got you thinking so hard?" Griggs bumped Bridger with his shoulder.

Bridger shrugged and tore a chunk off his homemade roll. "Just thinking about what day it is."

Griggs paused in the act of lifting his fork to his mouth. "You wanna talk about it?"

Bridger shook his head. "What I *want* is a cigarette. I either need to buy some more nicotine gum when we're in town later or I'm going to have to bust open a pack."

"I hear ya. I jumped all over Jimmy earlier for something he didn't even do. I told him I'd buy him a six-pack to make up for it."

"Do you think you'll stick with it after I leave?"

Griggs set down his fork and pushed his plate toward the center of the table. "Honestly? Probably not."

"Then why do it?" Bridger put his hand on Griggs' thigh.

Griggs threaded his fingers through Bridger's. "Because I know how important it is for you to quit."

Bridger didn't know what to say. Smoking was another thing he'd refused to hide from his parents since he was old enough to buy cigarettes. Although they'd bitched and tried to educate him on exactly what he was doing to his body, Bridger had continued to ignore them. It had taken one short conversation with Griggs to get him to at least attempt to quit.

Griggs released his hold on Bridger's hand. "You need to eat. We don't want a repeat performance of the other night."

"Hell, you've got Neil so freaked he makes me check my blood every two hours."

"He's a smart man."

Bridger forked another piece of meatloaf into his mouth. He knew they were supposed to have dinner in Red Lodge that evening at a later time than he was used to eating. He'd already decided to pack a small snack from the kitchen before he went back out with Neil.

"Is there anywhere on the ranch I can get cell phone reception?" he asked Griggs.

"Not reliably. Don't ask me why, but on a good day you can stand about forty paces from the northwest corner of the barn and get it. You might try, but I wouldn't count on it. Why? Someone you need to call?"

"My mom. Guess I can take my phone with me into Red Lodge later."

"She's probably missing you."

Bridger nodded. "Probably. What about your folks? Do you talk to them?"

"Sure. They still live in Seattle. I get out there from time to time, but I've been on my own for a while."

"And your sister, Rachel?"

"I've got two sisters. Rachel and Deanna. Rachel's a marketing rep for a pharmaceutical company and Deanna's married with four kids."

Bridger grinned. "Uncle Griggs."

Griggs shook his head. "Uncle Ethan. No one back home calls me by my last name, that'd be weird."

Ethan. Bridger rolled the name around in his head. "Ethan fits you. Why'd you start going by Griggs?"

"Wasn't really my choice. When I first started here there was another employee named Ethan, so they clarified things by calling me Griggs. Guess it stuck."

Bridger finished off his meatloaf and most of his green beans. "Would you rather I called you Ethan?"

Griggs smiled and leaned over to give Bridger a quick kiss. "No one would know who you were talking about."

"You and I would." Bridger followed Griggs' lips and kissed him, slipping his tongue inside for a brief taste. "You know, you taste a lot better since you quit smoking."

Griggs chuckled. "So do you. I guess that's another bonus."

The thought of stepping outside for a long drag on a cigarette made Bridger's mouth water. Damn, he'd loved to smoke. That he was attempting to quit because of the man at his side was proof of just how much Bridger liked him.

The other guests began to finish and filter out the door. Griggs nipped Bridger's ear lobe. "I'd better get going."

"The gate shouldn't take long to fix, so I should be back fairly early. Will you be around?"

"Yeah. We're done riding for the day. We have the meeting about the round-up at two, but other than that, we're letting them rest their sore asses in preparation for tomorrow."

Griggs stood and bent over for one more kiss. "I'll probably be in the barn when you get in. If you're a good boy, I'll let you shower with me before we go into town."

Bridger followed Griggs to the clean-up station and scraped his plate. Once they were outside, he pulled Griggs around to the side of the cookhouse and kissed his new lover properly.

"Bridger!" Neil called.

"We'll continue this later."

Griggs squeezed Bridger's ass. "You bet we will."

* * * * *

Bridger piled out of the van and waited with the others on the sidewalk. He couldn't get over the picturesque town of Red Lodge. The main street running down the center of town looked like something out of a movie with its quaint shops and restaurants.

Griggs came up behind him and turned him in the opposite direction. "There's the money shot."

"Damn." Snow covered mountains majestically stood guard over the town.

"Okay, everyone. Our reservations are in ninety minutes so just meet back here at seven," Griggs announced to the group.

Bridger fingered the phone in his jacket pocket. "Is there a quiet place I can check my emails and call home?"

Griggs glanced over his shoulder at Cody. "Are you going to check the reservations?"

Cody nodded. "On my way now."

"Thanks." Griggs took Bridger's hand and started walking down the sidewalk. "There's a great coffee shop down here."

"Starbucks?"

Griggs laughed. "Look around. There are no chain stores or restaurants of any kind in Red Lodge. The coffee shop is owned by a nice husband and wife."

Bridger was impressed by the warm, casual atmosphere of the coffee shop. He stepped up to the counter and ordered a simple black coffee and a honey nut muffin. "Do you have a favorite place to sit?"

Griggs picked up his coffee and led Bridger over to a deep chocolate brown sofa in front of the big windows. "I like to watch people coming and going."

Bridger set his coffee and muffin on the table and pulled out his cell phone. He wasn't surprised to see a large number of voicemails. He contemplated erasing them, but knew some of them were probably important. He held the phone up to Griggs. "Is this going to bother you?"

"Not at all."

The first thing he decided to do was call his mom. He wouldn't exactly categorize himself as a momma's boy, but he was closer to Beth Collinsford than he was to anyone else in his family.

"Hello?"

"Hey, Mom."

"Bridger! It's about time you called. I was starting to think they'd lost you on the trail somewhere."

Bridger smiled. His mom was the only one who knew where he'd really decided to vacation. His father thought he was in St. Thomas hanging with some of his college friends.

"They haven't abandoned me yet, Mom. This is the first chance I've had to come into town. The cell phone reception is pretty spotty on the ranch."

"Are you having fun?"

Bridger reached across the sofa and brushed Griggs' thigh. "I'm having the time of my life."

"Oh good. Are you getting this cowboy thing out of your system? Because you know how your father feels."

"I know perfectly well what Dad thinks of cowboys. And no, I'm not getting it out of my system." He didn't really want to get into the discussion with his mom over the phone and especially not in front of Griggs, but he needed to plant the seed. "I wish I could stay here forever, Mom."

"Well, we both know that's not possible. Maybe you can go back again?"

He felt Griggs squeeze his hand and looked up. Dark eyes of the man he was falling for stared back at him. Bridger was trying to figure out if it was a good stare or a bad stare when something his mother said caught his attention.

"What?"

"I said, your father told me to line up a decorator to redo the Junior Vice President's office for you."

Bridger closed his eyes and rested his head against the back of the couch. "I don't want to work in an office. You could decorate it any way you wanted and it still wouldn't make me happy."

"Oh, sweetie, we've talked about this before. Your father really does have your best interests at heart. I know you enjoy working outdoors, but it'll pass in time, you'll see."

"I need to go, but I'll be home for Sunday dinner, like always."

"I love you."

"Love you, too, Mom." Bridger pressed the end button and dropped the phone onto the cushion beside him. Screw his messages.

"You okay?"

Bridger shook his head. "She doesn't listen. Neither of them do."

"Were you serious about wanting to stay here?"

Bridger sat up and opened his eyes. "Of course I was." He shrugged. "But I don't know how to break away from them."

Griggs lifted Bridger's hand to his mouth and kissed it. "We'll figure it out."

Chapter Six
ಬ

Griggs was going over the plans for the mini-cattle drive with Neil when there was a tap on his shoulder. He turned and came face to face with James. "Yes?"

James glanced from Griggs to Neil and back to Griggs. "Can I talk to you for a minute?"

Griggs slapped Neil on the shoulder. "We should be ready to go in about five."

Neil nodded and walked off, his Australian Shepherd, Georgia, following close behind.

"What can I do for you?"

"I just want to apologize for stepping on your toes with Bridger. I don't get but one weekend a year to kick up my heels. I guess I pushed a little too hard."

Griggs put his hands on his hips. He didn't understand what kind of arrangement James might have with his wife, but he realized he wasn't in a position to judge. "I think Bridger's the one you should be apologizing to."

"Yeah, I know. I didn't want to approach him though until I'd talked to you."

Griggs couldn't keep the satisfied grin off his face. "Well we've talked."

"Right." James held out his hand and Griggs begrudgingly took it.

He watched the man walk off and shook his head. If there was even a small chance Bridger would be staying at the ranch, Griggs would have to make sure he let the guests know upfront that Bridger was his.

Griggs hoisted himself into the saddle and watched as James talked to his man. He noticed the distance Bridger kept from the married man. Hopefully Bridger wouldn't continue to have issues with the ranch guests, but if he did, Griggs wanted the younger man to know he always had his back.

"Mount up!" he yelled over the thrum of conversation.

Bridger shook James' hand and climbed on Jigsaw. Griggs absolutely loved the way Bridger looked in the saddle. Even the hard fucking Griggs had given the man earlier in the day didn't seem to change the way Bridger sat his horse.

Bridger smiled, flashing those tempting dimples. "I think James might be in love."

Griggs' good mood turned sour in an instant. "With you?"

"Hell no," Bridger said around a laugh. "With Rodney."

Surprised, Griggs scanned the gathered crowd until his gaze zeroed in on the two men. Yep. They certainly were making moon-eyes at each other. "As long as he stays the hell away from you, I don't care who he's fucking."

Bridger rolled his eyes and leaned across the distance for a quick kiss. "You're such a romantic."

Griggs shrugged. "I'm me, take me or leave me."

Bridger bit his bottom lip. "I'd like to take you, if you're offering."

At first Griggs thought Bridger meant the comment as a sexual innuendo, but the expression on Bridger's face told Griggs it was so much more than that. There was so much he wanted to say to the man he'd fallen in love with, but Neil and Cody were already heading the guests and other ranch hands toward the pasture.

He wanted to say something before the moment ended. "I'm definitely offering."

With the biggest, cheesiest smile he'd ever seen, Bridger rode off to catch up with the group, leaving Griggs with his own stupid grin plastered to his face.

* * * * *

Despite a few hiccups along the way, the guests managed to work with the regular ranch hands to get all the cattle into the grazing pasture. Griggs had made sure Bridger had been assigned to the group of guests he worked with.

As the last of the head were driven into the pasture, Griggs knew the real show was soon to begin. While rounding up the cattle, a few appeared lame for one reason or another. After the wet spring they'd had, Griggs wouldn't doubt a few of the cattle were showing early signs of foot rot.

The injured or sick cattle would need to be doctored in the field, which was common on a ranch the size of the Justice River. Griggs glanced at Bridger and gestured to Neil. "Why don't you go help Neil and show these folks how real cowboys do it."

With an enthusiastic nod, Bridger rode off toward the cowboss. Griggs steered Mick over to Deacon. "It went well."

"For the most part. We had riding issues with one group, but Ray babied them through it," Deacon said.

Neil and Bridger spoke for a few moments before cutting the first injured steer from the herd. Although the steer appeared lame earlier, it gave the men a run for their money. With their horses running at full speed, Bridger managed to get a rope around the steer's neck as Neil did the hardest part by roping the back legs.

Within moments they were both out of the saddle and running toward the steer, medicine pack draped over Neil's shoulder.

Beside him, Deacon whistled. "Neil wasn't joking when he said Bridger knew what the hell he was doing."

"Nope. He proved himself to me the first day," Griggs said with a great deal of pride in his voice.

"Grudgingly," Deacon added.

Griggs shrugged. "I resisted as long as I could." He took his eyes off Bridger long enough to realize Deacon was staring at him. "What?"

"You really like the kid, don't you?"

Griggs saw no reason to lie. "I think I've fallen in love with him."

"Ouch. So what're you going to do about it?"

"Beg you and Ray to give him a job and then beg him to take it."

"Well he's got a job if he wants it. That's pretty much a given. You should know that. The other half of the situation's in your hands."

After applying medicine and giving the steer an antibiotic injection, Neil and Bridger released the ropes. They mounted their horses and moved on to the next steer in need of attention.

Griggs caught sight of one of the guests with a small video camera, filming the skilled cowboys at work. He reminded himself to get a copy of the tape. Whether Bridger would stand up to his family or not, watching the man work was breathtaking.

"Does he feel the same about you?" Deacon asked, his eyes on the pair of cowboys.

"I don't know for sure, but I think so. I mean, I know he wants to stay, but I'm not sure if I mean enough to him to do so."

"What's the problem? College?" Deacon asked.

"His family." Griggs knew Bridger didn't want people to know who he really was, but if Deacon was planning to welcome him into the Justice River family, Griggs thought his boss had a right to know. "His dad's Theodore Collinsford."

"Damn." Deacon adjusted his hat further back on his head. "They're a big ranching family, though, so what's the problem?"

"According to Bridger, Theodore believes him to be above manual labor and has a cushy office in a high rise building all picked out for him," Griggs explained

"So the asshole's thumbing his nose at the very people who've made him a rich motherfucker?" Deacon shook his head. "I hate people like that."

"Yeah well, I think Bridger feels the same way as you, but he also loves his folks. He's stuck between what he wants to do and what he's supposed to do."

With the last of the cattle doctored, the gathered guests began clapping. Deacon started to ride off, but stopped and turned back toward Griggs. "Take it from someone who knows. Tell him how you feel before he leaves tomorrow."

Griggs had already figured that much out. He nodded his head at his boss and waited for Bridger to rejoin him. His thoughts went back to earlier that morning. After waking up, he'd pulled the blanket off the bed and dragged a still-sleepy Bridger out to the front porch. He'd settled them on the swing with Bridger in his lap and the blanket wrapped around them. As the horses were driven over the crest of the hill, he'd buried his cock deep into his lover's ass. It was the single finest morning of his life and he wanted more, a lot more.

* * * * *

"Thanks, Mother." Griggs took the big basket and gave the cook a kiss on the cheek.

He carried his aromatic bounty through the dining room and down to the small pasture. As he expected, he found Bridger sitting atop the fence with Harry's big head in his lap. "Thought I might find you out here."

Bridger glanced over his shoulder and smiled. "Just saying goodbye."

"You know, a few more months and Harry might actually let you put a saddle on him."

Bridger gasped. "Sacrilege. Harry should be ridden bareback or not at all."

Griggs set the basket down and leaned on the fence next to Bridger. "Think he'd really let you do it?"

Bridger continued to pet the wild mustang. "Yeah."

His Bridger's eyes went to the basket at Griggs' feet. "Smells like chicken."

"That's because it is. I asked Mother to pack it up for me. I thought I'd take you on a picnic."

"I thought we were all supposed to eat the last meal together?"

Griggs ran his hand up Bridger's leg to cup his cock. He gave the tempting mound of flesh a gentle, but firm, squeeze. "Maybe I don't want to share our last evening with a bunch of guests."

Immediately, pain laced Bridger's expression. He bent and gave Harry a quick kiss on the forehead before spinning around and holding out his arms.

Griggs lifted his lover from the fence and lowered him to the ground. "Is that a yes?"

"That's a yes. I need to stop by your place to get my kit though."

"No need. I already picked it up." Griggs held up the basket.

"Are we riding?"

"Kind of. Come on." He led Bridger by the hand toward the north pasture.

"No way!" Bridger squealed when he first saw Mick harnessed to a small buggy.

"It was Ray's grandpa's. He said we could use it."

Bridger ran his hands over the red leather seat before climbing on. "Asses must've been a lot smaller in the old days."

Griggs chuckled. As small as Bridger was, the two of them barely fit in the seat. He tapped the reins lightly against Mick's back and they took off. Griggs followed one of the grass and dirt truck paths over the hill. "How does a picnic beside the river sound?"

"Like heaven." Bridger released his hair from its ponytail before reaching up to untie the leather thong from Griggs' hair. "This is the way I like you best. Out in the middle of nowhere with your hair blowing in the evening breeze."

"Now who's getting poetic?"

"Me!" Bridger declared with enthusiasm.

* * * * *

Griggs pulled the buggy to a stop and jumped down. He didn't bother tying Mick, instead allowing his trusted horse to graze. He reached up and pulled Bridger into his arms. With the setting sun at his back, Griggs stared into the orange-hued face of the man he loved. "Don't go."

Bridger's Adam's apple bobbed several times before he spoke. "What happens if I give up everything and you get tired of me?"

"I won't. But I worry you'll start to regret giving up all that money."

"I won't. Besides, I have a little of my own. I was talking about alienating myself from my parents."

"Do you really think it'll come to that?" Griggs still didn't understand parents who put conditions on their love.

"I hope not, but I think it's a gamble I'm willing to take. This has been the happiest, most fulfilling week of my life."

"You know the winters suck in Montana. Just remember when you're freezing your ass off and the snow's hitting you square in the face how much you wanted to be a cowboy."

Bridger chuckled and rubbed his body against Griggs. "Those are probably the times I'd have to remind myself just how much I love the man who's waiting at home for me."

Griggs cupped Bridger's face in his hands. "Do you mean that?"

Bridger nodded. "I do."

Griggs kissed him, putting all his pent up feelings into each swipe of his tongue. He pulled back and stared into the eyes of his future. "I love you, too. Don't know how it happened. I certainly wasn't prepared to even like you, let alone fall completely head over heels."

Bridger hoisted himself up against Griggs' chest, wrapping his legs around Griggs' hips. "I've wanted you since the moment you offered me a light."

"I know. You were pretty obvious about it." Griggs laughed and squeezed Bridger's ass.

"Conceited much?"

Griggs' shrugged. "I've never had trouble finding men who wanted me to fuck 'em. But I knew that first night it was about more than having my cock up your ass."

Bridger groaned. "There goes that über-romantic side of you again."

After another deep kiss, Griggs set Bridger on his feet. "Let's eat before the chicken gets cold."

* * * * *

Bridger laughed as Griggs swiped the drops of cum off his stomach with a chicken leg. "Uhhh, using me as your dipping sauce now?"

"Mmm. Just making a memory. From now on every time I eat fried chicken I'll think of your taste."

Laughing so hard his stomach hurt, Bridger rolled over. He spotted movement out of the corner of his eye. "Don't even think about getting that greasy thing anywhere near my ass."

Griggs dropped down beside him and finished his chicken leg. "Wanna stay up all night?"

Bridger brushed the errant curls out of his face and studied his lover. Griggs was truly a goofball disguised as an incredibly sexy Native American stud. Bridger had a strong suspicion it was the reason he enjoyed Griggs' company, both in bed and out, more than any other man he'd ever spent time with.

"How old are you?" he finally asked.

"Thirty-six. Why, how old are you?" Griggs tossed the chicken bone into the picnic basket and held out his greasy fingers.

"Twenty-two." He opened his mouth and let Griggs slide his fingers into his mouth one by one. Once his lover was clean, Bridger scooted closer to tuck himself against Griggs' side. "Do you think we'll always have this much fun together?"

Griggs seemed to think about it for a few moments. "To be honest? No. I think there'll be times, especially during the winter, when we'll feel like killing each other. Luckily the ranch has a lot of room to roam and work out our problems. But you need to know going in that it won't always be easy. I can get grouchy. I don't like to change the sheets on the bed if I can get away with it. I usually open a new box of cereal before the old one's empty and if I get really drunk, I snore."

Bridger kissed Griggs' nipple. "Clean sheets are overrated. Who needs boxed cereal when I can get a hot breakfast in the cookhouse? And I pretty much pass out when I'm really drunk, so I won't hear you snore."

They settled into a companionable silence, holding each other and listening to the sounds of the bugs and frogs. Bridger knew they were both ignoring the biggest elephant in the room, but their evening had been so perfect, the thought of ruining it broke his heart.

"I'll talk to my parents at dinner on Sunday."

"You want me to go down there with you?"

Bridger rose up on one elbow. "You'd do that?"

"Of course I'd do that."

The offer warmed him. "Thanks, but I think it'll go better if I confront them on my own."

"You know, maybe that's part of the problem. Don't go in with a confrontation in mind. They're your parents. Just let them know what makes you happy."

"Sweet, naïve, Ethan. You know nothing about my father. He doesn't care what makes me happy. He cares about what makes him money."

"Then maybe you shouldn't care so much about what he thinks. You're not a commodity. You're his son."

Bridger didn't say it, but he wasn't so sure his father thought of him that way.

Chapter Seven

After taking care of the rest of the guests, Griggs pulled Bridger to the side, away from the security screeners. He tried to ignore the hum of the milling crowd of passengers coming and going from the airport. He pulled his lover against his chest and kissed him. "Letting you go is probably the hardest thing I've ever done in my life."

Bridger's eyes filled with tears. "Don't. I haven't cried yet in front of you and I don't want to start now."

"I've been thinking and maybe things would go over easier with your parents if you finished college first."

Bridger shook his head. "I have my bachelor's degree already. If I ever decide to go after my Masters in Business I can do it at MSU here in Billings." Bridger's head tilted to the side. "Or are you trying to tell me you've changed your mind?"

Griggs crushed Bridger even tighter against his chest despite a few dirty looks from people in the crowd. "No, I haven't changed my mind. I'm just afraid I'm being greedy. I want whatever's best for you."

"Then welcome me with open arms in a week or so."

Griggs nodded. "I can do that."

Bridger stepped back and slung his duffle bag over his shoulder. "I have one more favor to ask you."

"Anything."

"Good, because I want to bring my fifty-inch flat screen with me when I come back. I love you, honey, but you need to say goodbye to that nineteen-inch thing you watch."

Griggs chuckled. "You can bring anything you want back. Most of my things were in the house when I took the job."

"Cool." Bridger stood on his toes and kissed Griggs once more. "Love you. I'll call you when I get home."

"Love you, too." Griggs watched as the man he loved walked away. He knew in his heart Bridger would be back, but he wasn't sure how he was going to cope until he did.

Griggs waited until Bridger was through security and out of sight before walking out of the airport. The moment he was out the door, he reached into his pocket for a cigarette.

"Fuck!" Not only did he not have Bridger, now he didn't even have a vice to get him through until his lover came home.

* * * * *

The ringing phone woke Bridger the following morning. "Hello?"

"What time are you coming out to the ranch?" his mother asked.

Bridger stretched and glanced at the clock. He was surprised to see it was almost ten-thirty. He didn't bother telling his mom he'd stayed up until the wee hours of the morning talking to Griggs.

"Give me at least an hour. I didn't get to bed until late."

"Okay. Rosa's making pot roast because she knows it's your favorite."

"I'll be sure and thank her. What kind of mood is Dad in?"

"The usual. Why?"

"I just wondered. I'd better hop in the shower if I'm going to make it out there on time."

"I've missed you."

Bridger swallowed around the lump in his throat. "I've missed you, too, Mom."

* * * * *

After a quick shower, Bridger was on his way to the ranch. He'd always loved Collinsford Downs, but sadly the home he'd grown up in didn't hold the same appeal as it once did.

He stopped at the security gates and waited for the guards to let him inside. He definitely wouldn't miss that. Collinsford Downs was a combination working cattle ranch and media sideshow. Every time there was a story in one of the national magazines about Theodore Collinsford, it always included plenty of pictures of the distinguished grey-haired billionaire decked out in authentic-looking cowboy duds, riding one of his thoroughbreds.

Bridger parked his midnight blue sports car in front of the porch and got out. His nerves were on edge and he hoped he'd be able to get through dinner before blurting out his hopes for the future.

Upon entering the house, he was met by his mother who threw her arms around him. "You made it."

Bridger kissed his mother's youthful face. "Of course I made it, I told you I would." He glanced around the cavernous great room. "Where's Dad?"

Releasing her hold, Bridger's mother led him toward the dining room. "Would you like a drink before dinner?"

"Mom? Where's Dad?"

"He's in his office on an important conference call. He said he'd try to make it in time for dinner."

Bridger had to bite the inside of his cheek to keep from saying something he knew he'd regret. Sunday dinner had always been his mother's favorite activity of the week. Thankfully the drive from his small apartment in Austin to Collinsford Downs only took forty minutes, so he'd always made it a point to come home no matter what else was going on. Unfortunately, his father had never seen the importance of a familial weekly meal.

Bridger accepted a glass of white wine. As he looked at the sad, but resigned expression on his mother's face, he realized he wouldn't live a life like hers. Beth Collinsford had once been full of spirit, but the years of disappointments and eating alone had left her drained.

Without being prompted, Bridger set his glass down and leaned in to give his mom a hug. "I hope you know how much I love you."

When he pulled away, his mom's eyes were filled with tears. "You're leaving me, aren't you?"

"Please don't think of it that way. I'm not leaving you, but I am moving to Montana."

"You can't. You're all I have."

Bridger knew a truer statement had never been spoken. "I'm sorry, Mom, but I'm not your husband. Kids are supposed to grow up and find their own way in the world. That's all I'm asking for."

Beth covered her mouth and shook her head. "I'm sorry, baby, but I can't deal with this right now." She left the room without another word.

Bridger was left to figure out his next move. He picked up his glass of wine and walked down the hall to his father's office. He leaned against the wall and stared at the highly polished solid wood door. He wasn't allowed in the room, never had been. As he finished off his wine, he realized the door was a metaphor for everything that was wrong with his family.

With a deep breath, he reached down and grasped the knob only to find it was locked. *Locked?* What kind of husband and father locks his family out of his life?

Bridger sat the wine glass on the antique table beside the door on his way out of his boyhood home.

* * * * *

Griggs was leading a group of guests up the ranch road on their first ride when a large cloud of dust caught his eye. He spotted the big truck round the bend and quickly informed the guests to move to the grass beside the road.

He nudged Mick into a canter and took off toward the speeding truck. The closer he got to Bridger, the more nervous he became. It had only been a week since he'd held his lover, but Griggs knew how hard the last eight days had been on the younger man.

Bridger stopped the truck and got out, waiving like a crazy person as Mick closed the distance. Griggs reined Mick to a stop and jumped from his back. He ran the remaining ten yards and scooped Bridger off his feet and into his arms.

"God, I've missed you." He kissed Bridger before the man had a chance to say anything.

There was absolutely no finesse involved in the assault on his lover's mouth. Griggs alternated between dipping his tongue inside to taste the man he'd missed so much and nipping and scraping Bridger's lips with his teeth.

He broke the kiss and stared into the stormy eyes he'd been longing for. "You're early. I thought you said you'd be here tomorrow."

Bridger yawned. "I'd planned to stop somewhere along the way, but I just needed to get to you."

"You doing okay? Have you checked your blood sugar?"

Bridger smiled. "I'm fine. Just tired."

"Guess I'd better get you to bed then." Griggs grinned from ear to ear. He still couldn't believe Bridger had made the break from his old life in such a short time.

Bridger stared down the road. "New group?"

Griggs followed Bridger's gaze. The guests looked a little lost as they tried to keep their horses in line. "Yeah. Cody's not feeling well, so I told him I'd take them out by myself this evening."

"Why don't you finish up and I'll meet you back at the house?"

Something in Bridger's voice bothered Griggs. "Are you sure you're okay? Did you talk to your mom before you left?"

"A little. She still feels like I'm abandoning her." Bridger shook his head. "I don't feel like going into it now. I just want a hot shower and a warm bed."

Griggs gave Bridger another quick kiss. "Okay, baby. I should be there in about an hour."

Bridger nodded and pulled away.

"Let me get back to the guests before you drive by."

"I can do that." Bridger grinned as he got back into the truck. He rolled his window down as Griggs mounted up. "By the way, I missed you, too."

It was the first smile Griggs had seen from Bridger in a week and just the sight warmed his heart. "I love you," he mouthed.

"You, too," Bridger answered back.

* * * * *

Bridger was sound asleep when a cold, nude body pressed against him. "Damn. Is it really that cold out there?"

Griggs kissed Bridger's neck. "No. You're just incredibly warm. I didn't mean to wake you."

"Yeah you did."

Griggs chuckled. "Yeah. I did."

Bridger rolled over to face his lover. He threw his leg over Griggs' hip and scooted as close as he could. "I noticed you haven't changed the sheets since I left."

Griggs' licked at Bridger's lips. "I couldn't bring myself to do it. These smell like us. I like it."

"They're getting a little…crusty."

Griggs ran his hand down Bridger's back to his ass. "Promise that you'll be with me every night from here on out and I'll change 'em."

Bridger hiked his leg up higher on Griggs' torso and wiggled his butt until he felt Griggs' fingers find his already stretched and lubed hole.

Griggs' eyes widened. "You trying to tell me something?"

"No, but my ass is. It's been awfully lonely. I think it'd like some company." Bridger scraped Griggs' lower lip with his teeth. "When I went to the doctors last week to get my final checkup and paperwork transferred, I had him test me at the same time."

Griggs smiled as he sawed two fingers in and out of Bridger's ass. "Are you telling me you want to do away with condoms?"

Bridger nodded. "You've already shown me your most recent test results. And since I don't plan on being with another lover for the next fifty years or so, I think I'd like to feel nothing but you."

"Fifty years? You plan on skipping out on me when you're in your seventies?"

Bridger groaned as Griggs replaced his fingers with the head of his bare cock. "I don't plan on going anywhere, but you might find a sexy sixty-year-old you decide you like better."

Griggs eased his cock several inches. "Not possible."

Despite stretching himself earlier and Griggs' finger play, Bridger felt the burn of the thick cock as it slid in. He'd happily accept the pinch of pain if it meant becoming one with the man he loved.

Bridger tried to block out the anguish of the last few days as he gave himself over to the pleasures of being fucked by the strong wrangler. "Deeper."

Griggs buried his cock to the root and pulled Bridger on top of him. "Better?"

"It will be." Bridger braced his feet on either side of Grigg's hips and sat up. He gazed at Griggs, happier than he'd ever been. The new position plunged Griggs' cock even deeper. "Oh, shit."

Bridger swiveled his hips several times before leaning down for a kiss. He swirled his tongue around the interior of Griggs' mouth as his body accommodated the extra depth of his lover's shaft. Had he ever felt so completely filled? "You feel good."

"I can feel even better." Griggs grasped Bridger's ass in his hands and began to thrust in and out.

With his body tilted forward, Bridger felt his cock rub against the hard ridges of Griggs' abdomen. *Oh, yeah, right there.* With each thrust, Griggs managed to hit Bridger's prostate. Bridger gripped the sheets in his fist as he struggled to breathe through the onslaught of pleasure. It was too much and not enough at the same time. The slide of his cock against the lightly furred stomach of Griggs only added to the sweet torture.

As Griggs pace increased, so did the decibel level in the room. The sounds of skin slapping against skin had always been one of his favorite melodies, even more so when added to the grunts and groans coming from Griggs. Bridger knew he could happily hear that tune for the rest of his life.

"I'm going to shoot," Bridger warned.

Griggs growled as he hammered Bridger's hole with his thick shaft. The assault on Bridger's prostate was too much to resist and he shot, calling out his lover's name.

"Ethan!" Bridger yelled.

Griggs' rhythm faltered as his chest and chin were painted by strings of Bridger's thick, white cum. Bridger began to wonder if he'd ever stop coming. Never had a lover fucked him to the point of passing out, but Griggs was well on his way of doing just that. Bridger gulped in air in an effort to stay coherent as the final jets of cum left his body.

"Bridger!" Griggs howled to the ceiling as he came.

Never in his life had Bridger had sex without a condom, but it seemed so incredibly right to feel his ass being filled with Griggs' warm seed.

Bridger collapsed on Griggs' chest, the sticky fluid bonding him further to his man. The smells in the small room were almost overwhelming. He grinned as he realized he wasn't the only one who'd come more than usual.

Griggs released his hold on Bridger's ass and wrapped his arms around him. "Love you."

"Love you." Bridger started to squirm as the cum began to leak out of his hole from around Griggs' softening cock. "Tickles."

Griggs reached down and rubbed the thick cream with his fingers, smearing it over both of them.

Bridger moaned. Being painted with Griggs' cum was the most erotic thing he'd ever had a lover do to him.

"I'll never be able to describe what that felt like," Griggs panted.

"What? Fucking without a condom?" Bridger asked.

"Yeah," Griggs answered.

Bridger bit his lower lip. He realized there was a very important part of their sex-life they'd never discussed. "Do you like to get fucked?"

"Me?" Griggs face pinched. "Not really, but I don't want to be selfish about always being on top either."

Bridger grinned and shook his head. "I knew there was a reason we were perfect for each other. I've only fucked one person and I didn't understand the appeal. Maybe I like being taken care of? I don't know."

"Well then it's a damn good thing I like taking care of you."

Bridger rested his cheek against Griggs' chest and yawned. "I think we could use another shower, but I'm too tired to get up."

"Was the drive bad?"

"I didn't mind the driving as much as the loneliness. It gave me way too much time to think."

"Well, you didn't turn around and head back to Austin, so I guess that's a good sign, right?"

Bridger kissed his lover's chest. "Not being with you was never an option. I just wish my parents didn't hate me because of the choices I've made."

"They don't hate you. They may not understand them and they're probably pretty angry about them, but I can guarantee they don't hate you for them."

"Easy for you to say, you didn't see the look my dad gave me the one and only time he talked to me about it." He shook his head. "He honestly doesn't understand why anyone would choose this life."

Griggs ran his hands over Bridger's back. "Give it time, babe."

It was the same advice he'd given himself at least once an hour since he'd left Austin. He knew it might very well be true, but there was a large part of him that felt adrift without an anchor.

With his arms wrapped around Bridger, Griggs rolled them until Bridger was on his back. "You stay here. I'll go get a nice warm washcloth to clean you up."

As Bridger watched Griggs' cute ass walk out of the bedroom, he realized he wasn't adrift at all. He had a man he loved and a job he'd been born to do.

"Hey, Griggs?"

The water shut off and Griggs came back into the room. "Yeah, babe?"

"You ever think of getting an anchor tattooed on your ass?"

Epilogue

Griggs was in the middle of helping their resident handyman replace a broken window in the Jackson's Ridge cabin when he spotted a big black limousine pull up in front of the cookhouse. "According to Jeff and Caleb that's exactly what happened. Caleb's just lucky he wasn't hurt worse than he was."

"Are we expecting the president?" Tyson chuckled, noticing the limousine.

Griggs knew immediately who sat behind the darkened windows. "Worse. That's Bridger's father, Theodore."

"Seriously? If Bridger comes from money like that, what the hell is he doing working as a hired hand?"

"Have you seen Bridger lately? The man hasn't stopped grinning since he moved here three weeks ago. He lives to get dirty."

Tyson chuckled again. "I can understand that. This place has been the best thing that's ever happened to me."

"I guess I'd better go talk to him. It doesn't appear that he's going to get out of the car on his own."

As he neared the car, the back window slid down and Griggs came face to face with the man who'd caused Bridger so much pain. "Mr. Collinsford."

The older man's silver eyebrows lifted. "You know who I am?"

"Of course. I'm Ethan Griggs, Bridger's partner."

"You're the one who sent the package."

"Yes, sir." Griggs took several steps back. "Are you getting out?"

Theodore seemed to study Griggs for several moments before alighting from the car. Griggs didn't know it for a fact, but he had a feeling it was the first time the man had opened his own door in years.

Once Theodore stood in front of him, Griggs reached out his hand, surprised when Theodore readily took it. "I'd like to thank you for sending me that video."

"I thought you had a right to see your son at work." The video one of the earlier guests had shot was even better than Griggs had hoped. It truly showed Bridger's superior roping and riding skills in action. More than the physical show on display, it was the expression on Bridger's face that had left Griggs mesmerized.

He knew as soon as he'd watched it he needed to send it to Bridger's parents. They deserved to see their son truly happy.

"Bridger's always been so small. I had no idea..." Theodore shook his head. He cleared his throat and glanced around the ranch. "Is he around?"

"Yep. I guess before I take you to him, I need to know what's going on. He's happy here and I won't have you upsetting him again."

Theodore's eyes narrowed for several moments as he seemed to size up Griggs. He finally nodded. "Fair enough. I wanted to let him know he was welcome back home anytime. There are a few other things I need to talk to him about, but I'll let *him* tell you if he wants to."

"He's been spending most of his off time working with a wild Mustang named Harry." Griggs started walking toward Harry's small pasture.

"How far is it?" Theodore asked.

"Not far." Griggs couldn't keep the grin off his face at the thought of the billionaire businessman ruining his thousand-dollar shoes in the dirt of the ranch road.

He rounded the small stand of trees and stopped. When Theodore started to walk by him, he reached out and grabbed the man's arm. "Hang on."

"Why?"

Griggs gestured to the pasture. "That horse has never been ridden before. Most of the hands can't get anywhere near the fence without Harry going crazy."

Theodore actually started to smile. "That boy always did have a way with animals. Guess I should've known he'd turn out the way he did."

Griggs looked back at the sight of his lover riding Harry, bareback, around the pasture, his black curls lifting in the breeze. He knew if Bridger could take on Satan's Spawn and win, he could take on anything.

* * * * *

Griggs collapsed beside Bridger, rubbing his chest as he tried to regulate his breathing. It didn't matter how many times he made love to Bridger, it only seemed to intensify.

"Mmm. That was nice," Bridger whispered.

"More than nice. I think you might've squeezed my dick off with that tight ass of yours," Griggs panted.

Bridger chuckled and reached down to grasp Griggs' now-flaccid cock. "Nope, still there."

Although Griggs wished his cock was up for another round, he knew it wasn't going to happen, at least for another hour at least. He rolled to his side and curled himself around Bridger. "I'm glad you were able to work things out with your dad."

Bridger snorted. "I wouldn't call it worked out. But at least he's tolerating my career choice. I think he still hopes I'll change my mind and join the corporate world, but we both know that won't happen."

Griggs placed a soft kiss on Bridger's neck. "They love you. Faced with the choice of losing you, I'm not surprised your dad amended his earlier position."

"Yeah," Bridger murmured. "I just can't believe how hard I tried over the years to get him to listen to me. It wasn't until I walked away that he finally heard me." Griggs knew Bridger and his dad had a long road ahead of them, but hopefully Bridger's happiness would prove to his family he'd made the right career choice. Griggs also knew he would play a large part in helping to make Bridger happy. It was a job Griggs was more than eager to perform.

"I think your dad seeing you on Harry went a long way in convincing him," Griggs said.

Bridger rolled to face Griggs. "Really? Because I happen to think your protectiveness towards me helped the most. Dad even said if he had to let his son out into the world, he was happy I had a man like you by my side."

Griggs smiled. It was a nice thing to hear. He rubbed his hand over Bridger's back. *And an even better thing to feel.* "Love you."

"Forever," Bridger whispered as his eyes slowly closed.

Griggs knew he should get up and clean his lover before allowing him to fall asleep but for the moment, he couldn't imagine letting Bridger go long enough to do that. He held Bridger in his arms, promising to do whatever it took to help the man succeed in whatever life handed him.

Also by Carol Lynne

eBooks:

Feels So Right
Finnegan's Promise
Gio's Dream
Harvest Heat
Men in Love 1: Branded by Gold
Men in Love 2: Ben's Wildflower
Men in Love 3: Open to Possibilities
Men in Love 4: Completing the Circle
Men in Love 5: Going Against Orders
Men in Love 6: Tortured Souls
Necklace of Shame
Never Too Old
No Longer His
Riding the Wolf
Saddle Up and Ride 1: Reining in the Past
Saddle Up and Ride 2: Bareback Cowboy
Sex With Lex
Sunshine, Sex and Sunflowers

Print Books:

Down Under Temptation
Finnegan's Promise
Forbidden Love
Men in Love 1 & 2: Branded by Love

Men in Love 3: Open to Possibilities
Men in Love 4: Completing the Circle
Naughtiest Nuptials *(anthology)*
Protected Love
Taboo Treats *(anthology)*

About Carol Lynne
ಐ

I've been a reading fanatic for years and finally at the age of 40 decided to try my hand at writing. I've always loved romance novels that are just a little bit naughty so naturally my books tend to go just a little further. It's my fantasy world after all.

When I'm not being a mother to a five-year-old and a six-year-old, you can usually find me in my deep leather chair with either a book in my hand or my laptop.

ಐ

The author welcomes comments from readers. You can find her website and email address on her author bio page at www.ellorascave.com.

Tell Us What You Think

We appreciate hearing reader opinions about our books. You can email us at Service@ellorascave.com (when contacting Customer Service, be sure to state the book title and author).

Why an electronic book?

We live in the Information Age—an exciting time in the history of human civilization, in which technology rules supreme and continues to progress in leaps and bounds every minute of every day. For a multitude of reasons, more and more avid literary fans are opting to purchase e-books instead of paper books. The question from those not yet initiated into the world of electronic reading is simply: *Why?*

1. *Price.* An electronic title at Ellora's Cave Publishing runs anywhere from 40% to 75% less than the cover price of the exact same title in paperback format. Why? Basic mathematics and cost. It is less expensive to publish an e-book (no paper and printing, no warehousing and shipping) than it is to publish a paperback, so the savings are passed along to the consumer.
2. *Space.* Running out of room in your house for your books? That is one worry you will never have with electronic books. For a low one-time cost, you can purchase a handheld device specifically designed for e-reading. Many e-readers have large, convenient screens for viewing. Better yet, hundreds of titles can be stored within your new library—on a single microchip. There are a variety of e-readers from different manufacturers. You can also read e-books on your PC or laptop computer. (Please note that Ellora's Cave does not endorse any specific brands.

You can check our website at www.ellorascave.com for information we make available to new consumers.)

3. *Mobility.* Because your new e-library consists of only a microchip within a small, easily transportable e-reader, your entire cache of books can be taken with you wherever you go.

4. *Personal Viewing Preferences.* Are the words you are currently reading too small? Too large? Too... ANNOYING? Paperback books cannot be modified according to personal preferences, but e-books can.

5. *Instant Gratification.* Is it the middle of the night and all the bookstores near you are closed? Are you tired of waiting days, sometimes weeks, for bookstores to ship the novels you bought? Ellora's Cave Publishing sells instantaneous downloads twenty-four hours a day, seven days a week, every day of the year. Our webstore is never closed. Our e-book delivery system is 100% automated, meaning your order is filled as soon as you pay for it.

Those are a few of the top reasons why electronic books are replacing paperbacks for many avid readers.

As always, Ellora's Cave welcomes your questions and comments. We invite you to email us at Service@ellorascave.com or write to us directly at Ellora's Cave Publishing Inc., 1056 Home Avenue, Akron, OH 44310-3502.

Discover for yourself why readers can't get enough of the multiple award-winning publisher Ellora's Cave. Be sure to visit EC on the web at www.ellorascave.com to find erotic reading experiences that will leave you breathless. You can also find our books at all the major e-tailers (Barnes & Noble, Amazon Kindle, Sony, Kobo, Google, Apple iBookstore, All Romance eBooks, and others).

www.ellorascave.com

CPSIA information can be obtained at www.ICGtesting.com
Printed in the USA
LVOW081839280613

340740LV00002B/358/P